RATNA TRANSLATION SERIES

AFTER YESTERDAY

AND OTHER STORIES

APPADURAI MUTTULINGAM

TRANSLATED FROM TAMIL BY
PADMA NARAYANAN

EDITED BY
DEBRA BLACK

RATNA BOOKS

Originally published in Tamil by Kalachuvadu Publications in April 2013
and July 2015
Original Tamil copyright © Appadurai Muttulingam

First published in English translation 2017
English translation copyright © Appadurai Muttulingam 2017

ISBN   978-93-5290-747-2 (POD)

Published by **RATNA BOOKS**
An imprint of Ratna Sagar P. Ltd.
Virat Bhavan, Mukherjee Nagar Commercial Complex
Delhi 110009, India
www.ratnabooks.in

APPADURAI MUTTULINGAM was born in Kokuvil, Sri Lanka. A chartered accountant by profession, his literary career started at the age of nineteen when he won the first prize in the All Ceylon Tamil Short Story Competition conducted by *Thinakaran*, a national newspaper. He has published eleven short story collections, six essay collections, two interview collections, two novels and edited an anthology of book reviews. He has won the Tamil Nadu Government (India) Award for *Vamsa Viruthi*, Sri Lanka Government Literary Award for *Vadakku Veethi*, Ananda Vikatan India Award 2012 and S.R.M. University (India) Literary Award 2013. He also won the Markham City Council, Canada Literary Award 2014. A selection of short stories translated into English under the title *Inauspicious Times* was published in 2008. His short story 'The American Girl' was included in the book *Many Roads through Paradise*, an anthology published by Penguin Books in 2014. The same story was included in *Uprooting the Pumpkin*, an anthology published by Oxford University Press in 2016. He lives with his wife Ranjini in Markham, Canada.

PADMA NARAYANAN is a Chennai-based writer and translator. Her translations of short stories have been included in an anthology brought out by the British Council. Her other translations include two novellas by the Tamil writer La Sa Ra (Katha), *Ashes and Wisdom* by Indira Parthasarathy (Indian Writing) and *Inauspicious Times* by Appadurai Muttulingam.

EDITOR

DEBRA BLACK is a writer, editor and yoga and meditation teacher. She was a reporter and feature writer at the *Toronto Star* for 28 years. Prior to her stint at the *Star*, she worked as a freelance magazine and newspaper writer for Canadian and international publications; a reporter and editor at Canadian Press; a radio and television reporter for the Canadian Broadcasting Corporation in Saskatchewan and as an editor at an alternative television station and newspaper.

'These stories by Appadurai Muttulingam are serious, funny and piercingly honest. Through retelling the stories of the ordinary, common man in his daily struggles for survival, the characters in these stories force us to take a second look at ourselves; they force us to consider ourselves in the shoes of folks who face social, economic and political hardships in their lives.

'Appadurai Muttulingam's writing style reminds one of R.K. Narayan. He uses terse, sinewy sentences and doesn't bother the reader with gratuitous language or details. His mission is to narrate a story, and he does it in a take-it-or-leave-it manner of folk tales, in which logic and superfluous information are sacrificed for the sake of a delightful read and a universal message.'

Contents

one

Unexpected

L ET ME TELL YOU about the first bewildering experience that I had in Africa. Even after all these years, it refuses to fade away. Recently, I wondered why I hadn't written about it earlier. Is it because I thought no one would believe it? I don't know. Or maybe, it is destined to come out only now. Perhaps. Anyway, here is what happened.

It was only a few years before my arrival that Sierra Leone had won its independence from British rule. So the country was still very British. For instance, it still used the British pound for its currency even though it had created a new currency and named it 'Leone'. Two leones made one pound and both currencies were in use in Sierra Leone at that time. Whatever you could get in England, you got in Sierra Leone. The upper class of Sierra Leone spoke, acted and dressed like the British. It seemed to me as though the people were fairly prosperous. Nowhere was poverty overtly visible. In

1

the village where I was posted, people spent their evenings revelling in music and dance.

When I left Ceylon, which is called Sri Lanka now, the imports into the country had stopped and exports had dwindled, and essential commodities were in short supply. You had to stand in line at five in the morning to buy your bread. For milk, you had to be there at four, and if you needed onions, you had to be there at least by three for you to have any chance of buying them. We needed to get a minister's reference just to be able to get milk powder for our baby. Coming from such an austere background at home, it was no wonder that we were entranced by the sight of shops filled with all kinds of stuff in Africa. It felt like we had landed right in London. There were no TVs in Ceylon then, but we found them everywhere in Sierra Leone. Whereas Ceylon had only two types of cars – Austin 30 and Morris Minor, Mercedes Benz was a most common sight in Africa.

I should have done some serious thinking before I agreed to my wife's suggestion that we send a few things to Ceylon in a parcel. Making a parcel of some things that were then not available in Ceylon, I went to the only post office in the village. It didn't even have a sign that said 'Post Office'. It was just a small room enclosed by long iron bars. At first glance, it looked like a prison. A cheap chair and a table with a few small objects on it were the only things in the room. A man of about fifty/fifty-five years of age stood behind the table. It was not all that hard to guess that he was the postmaster, clerk and postman, all rolled into one. He had close-cut his curly hair and his lips were slightly upturned, like a horse's. He wore a long, loose shirt and pants that were longer than his legs; the extra cloth lay curled up at his feet.

I greeted him in his language. The African exchange of greetings can be very long. Thankfully, I had memorized them, so I could now follow the protocol. Five minutes went by as we exchanged greetings. I noticed that there was a dog lying inside the room, with a child sleeping on top of it. The dog seemed to be asleep as well. The man was the only one awake. He was standing there chewing kola nut and, for some reason, it had not occurred to him to sit on the empty chair.

I had heard of this man from my colleagues at work. He was the richest man of the village. He had sold off his four daughters successfully – each for a good price. He owned a hundred goats and over fifty cows. His sons-in-law visited him now and then, and he would ask each of them: 'Which girl of mine did you marry?'

'The fourth one.'

'How many goats did you give me?'

The son-in-law would mention a number. The man's status would thus be determined and ministrations to him would follow accordingly. This post office job was a mere pastime for him. On any given day he would have one or two customers like me. That meant he was in no hurry to be done with me.

By nodding his head he wanted to know what I needed. I lifted up and showed him the parcel I had in my hand. He asked me where I wanted to send it. I replied 'Ceylon'. Uncomprehending, he asked me the question again. I repeated 'Ceylon'. He picked up a large book and scanned the pages first from left to right, and then from right to left, and declared, 'There is no Ceylon here.'

I took the book through the railings, searched for 'Ceylon' and showed him the name written in very small print. Reluctant to argue further, he accepted that there, indeed, was a country called by that unusual name.

He asked for the parcel to be handed over to him. As the package could not go through the railings, he opened the door, came out and took the parcel from me, and began to weigh it on some contraption that vaguely resembled a balance. After performing what looked like some tricks, he finally noted down the weight. He then took out a long book, pored over its pages, made all sorts of calculations, arrived at a figure, and finally looked up. I could feel my stomach churning, my heart beating faster in anticipation of his pronouncement. Without any further delay, he announced: 'Forty leones.'

'What?!'

I cried. The dog woke up with a start and the baby rolled off its back, but continued to sleep.

Forty leones were equal to twenty British pounds. Even if I sold my child like the legendary king Harishchandra had, I wouldn't be able to raise that kind of money.

'The things in the parcel cost only five leones,' I said to him. But I regretted it instantly, for he immediately asked me to declare the items in the parcel. I listed the items one by one, feeling a sense of shame as I did it. The man's face mirrored the thoughts that were passing through his mind.

Who takes the trouble of sending such paltry items to another country, Ceylon, a country that was not even found in his book? Honestly, I was not sending any essential items. In fact, humankind could still survive rather comfortably without them: 'A whistle, Donald Duck, a talking doll…'

He interrupted me, 'Talking doll? What would that be? Why would you want to send that?'

'Friend, ours is a democratic country; dolls are allowed to speak their minds,' I said.

Just then, a colleague of mine saw me and rushed in uninvited and, without a word to me, said something to the postmaster in their language and the postmaster replied. My friend spoke some more, to which the postmaster said something in reply. This went on for a while, and it seemed that they had completely forgotten about my presence. I butted in and asked my friend, 'What did you tell him?'

He had informed the postmaster that I was a senior officer and some consideration should be shown to me. I asked him what the postmaster had said in reply.

'Even a king has to bend while throwing up,' was the answer.

'That's all right, I can manage by myself. Thanks for your help,' I said and sent him on his way.

The postmaster suddenly asked me, 'What's today's date?', as if I was responsible for that too. He needed to know the right date to stamp the parcel. I told him it was Friday, but he picked up the calendar on his table and tore the top sheet off. It became Wednesday. He tore off another sheet and it became Thursday. When the next sheet was torn off, it showed the correct day – Friday, and the date I had given him was right. Having successfully established the date, he stretched his hand through the railings and said, 'Forty leones,' again.

I told him, 'There must be some mistake in your register. This small parcel should not cost all that much to be mailed.'

'Who is the authority here?' he raised his voice. He spat out his words like he was spitting out some insects that had entered his mouth.

Summoning up a respectful tone, I said, 'It'd be kind of you if you could check again.'

Once again, he fetched the register that he had apparently spent so many days to prepare, the one that was decipherable only to him, and wrote down the number '40' on a piece of paper and showed it to me. The number was now recorded on a piece of paper, so it must be right! I said, 'Nowhere else in the world is the charge so high.'

'This is the minimum charge. Your parcel will go to your country by sea. Any rate less than this is not feasible. Already the postal department is running at a loss,' he said.

'I am also running at a loss,' I pleaded. He did not pay any heed to my words and was rolling with his tongue the kola nut from one cheek to the other.

'Can I talk to your supervisor?' I asked.

He waved his hands expansively, as if warding off mosquitoes, and said, 'I am the boss.'

'Then what about a meeting with the boss's boss?'

'I am that as well.'

It was then that I realized for the first time that I was standing in front of the all-powerful postal authority of Sierra Leone. I picked up my parcel and walked away. There was no way I could go back home and declare to my wife the fate of the parcel. So I decided to fling the parcel into the woods on my way home. Let the elephants and foxes blow on the whistle and the colobus monkeys dance to the tune. In any case, even if it was sent, the parcel would never have reached its destination. So, a small lie to my wife would save the situation, I reasoned. I had just made up my mind to put my thoughts into action when the postmaster came running after me, shouting.

'Why do you get angry over such petty things? Come, come.'

He spoke as if he were inviting me to a wedding feast, and I accepted it, wondering what new thoughts were forming inside his head. That was how the whistle, Donald Duck and the talking doll were saved from the ignominy that was about to befall them.

I saw that the postmaster was in the habit of opening his mouth wide even to utter a small word. Lost in observing his mouth, I didn't hear what he was saying: 'Okay! What will you give me for the parcel?' I was taken aback, but without showing it I mentioned a figure. He came up with another number. The haggling went on for a while and gradually, a settlement was reached. Even before I paid him the agreed amount, he was sticking the stamps on the parcel and stamping them with a seal. 'You may go now,' he bid me farewell. The baby suddenly sat up, looked at me and gave a bright smile. The dog shook himself and stood wagging its tail furiously. Somehow they seemed to know that the business of the day had been concluded.

I came home and told my wife that the parcel had been dispatched, although I was sure that it would never reach its destination. But a month later we received a letter from Ceylon informing us that the parcel had, in fact, arrived in Colombo.

That was the first surprise I encountered in Africa. But, in retrospect, I feel that it pales in comparison to all the others that were to follow.

two

The Witch's Sister

'THAT WEDNESDAY IS an unforgettable day in my life. It's because no one died that day. I would even say that it was the luckiest day in the last six months. Usually one, two, five or, at times, even ten of us died every day. That's when I decided to leave the country, to get away somehow,' said the refugee. He sat shrunk and crouched in the middle of a chair with neither of his arms touching the armrests. Amanda listened to him, sitting on a sofa with her legs stretched.

The day before, when Amanda met him outside Toronto's Loblaws supermarket, he'd looked about twenty-five years old and had shown her a scrap of paper with an advertisement on it, and she'd read it without betraying any particular interest. On it was written, 'I am a refugee. I can do all kinds of work around a house – maintenance, gardening, redoing the driveway and so on, at very little cost.'

Now, there were plenty of repairs to be done at Amanda's house. So she gave the refugee her address and asked him to come over the next day. The walls needed to be repainted. He came at the appointed hour, carrying in his hands all the tools required for the work, and on his lips plenty of strange stories to tell. She liked him.

The refugee worked at Amanda's house for several days. He repaired the driveway, he did gardening and talked to himself and laughed quite often. Amanda noticed that his eyes disappeared whenever he laughed. One day Amanda said that she wanted a bookshelf made. There was no space any more in any of the other bookshelves, and her books lay scattered on the floor. She read a lot, and did not go out to work. When she was not reading, she was typing away on her computer. Like a diligent woodpecker, she let her fingers peck at the keys at 120 words per minute. When she took breaks, she supervised his work. She liked the shelf he made with planks bought to exact measurements. The refugee worked for her three or four days a week.

One day he asked her, 'Ma'am, can you help me with something?' She was surprised. Until then, he had never asked questions; he had only replied. She asked him what it was about. He needed a credit card. The bank had rejected his application and if she could stand guarantee for him, he might get one. Amanda went with him to meet the bank manager and deposited $500 as guarantee. His joy at getting the credit card was inexplicable. 'Ma'am, we have to celebrate this occasion; will you have a cup of coffee with me?' She agreed. Later, she marvelled at the pride he displayed when he paid for the coffee with his new card. She hadn't asked him any questions about his past yet.

But she was curious and eventually asked, 'How did you come into this country?'

'There is a war on in my country,' he told her. 'I fought in the army for six years. It was not uncommon to see at least one soldier die every day. At one stage, I just got a fake passport made and came into this country. My refugee status has been refused, but the lawyer has appealed that decision.'

Amanda looked at him in amazement. His face was so perfect, not a flaw to be fixed. Uncomfortable under her intense stare, he smiled and lowered his head. Hair kept short and close to his pate; well-formed shoulders with their muscles bulging and moving as he worked with his hands; a taut and drawn-in middle; jeans and discoloured shirt that fitted him perfectly, clinging to the contours of his body... She saw it now. There could be no doubt that he'd been a soldier.

'Who are you, ma'am?' he asked suddenly.

'Me? Maybe the sister of a witch.'

'You are making fun of me! What work do you do? I see you all the time in front of your computer. Has that got anything to do with your job?'

'I work in a publishing company. My job is to read and assess manuscripts. The company publishes only those books that I recommend for publication. The rest get rejected.'

'Then your work must be quite interesting. You get to read

11

all those good novels for free, and you get paid for it. Some plum job it is!'

'That is not true. Some novels are so bad that finishing them is a punishment in itself. But you know how writers are. They always think that they have produced nothing but extraordinary work.'

'Have you read anything good recently, ma'am?'

'A book arrived yesterday. I thought of you when I read it. It is the story of a refugee.'

'Interesting! Can you tell me more about it, ma'am?'

'A refugee comes into America from Latvia. He does not have any kind of skill. He is unable to last in a job for more than two days. He tries everything – building roads, assisting in the kitchen, stacking boxes in huge departmental stores, but nothing suits him. He works for just ten days a month and manages to get by. One day his boss gives him a big box and asks him to deliver it to a rich man's house. Though it happens to be the middle of the night, the boss insists that the box be delivered immediately.

'That wealthy man lives all alone in his huge villa. When the refugee arrives with the box, he sees the man sitting there, drinking red wine in somewhat subdued light. The rich man accepts the box, but makes no attempt to open it. He is in very high spirits and asks the delivery man to have a glass of wine with him. The man agrees and sits down for a drink.

'The delivery man just takes a sip and exclaims, "Ah! This is Amarone." The rich man is surprised. "So you know about wines?" he asks. "Yes, a little," replies the delivery man.

'The rich man goes down into his cellar and brings out another expensive bottle of wine. The man takes a sip, ponders for a few minutes and says, "Bordeaux, Cheval Blanc – 1998."

'The rich man cannot believe his ears and embraces the man in joy. The rich man is so happy he offers the delivery man a job at his winery the very same day. He prospers in his career gradually and one day becomes a partner to his boss. He also has an affair with his boss's wife, and eventually marries her. The story ends there. He rues his treacherous act for the rest of his life and is not able to enjoy his wealth. The act bothers him over and over again. What would have happened to him if he had not met that rich man that midnight? He never seems to get any answers though.'

'That's a sad story,' said the refugee. She replied, 'Is it sorrow or treachery that it speaks of? There will be, at least, one act of betrayal in every man's life. The betrayer should forget, and the betrayed should forgive.'

The refugee asked hesitantly, 'Is there betrayal in your life, ma'am? Why aren't you married?'

'I did marry. My husband divorced his first wife and married me. We were together for ten years. Once my elder sister visited me and was with us for just a few days. My husband left me and ran off with her. They are now married, I hear. Marriage is a good thing, I suppose, but you should not make a habit of it.'

The refugee was silent. She did not say anything either.

She planned to have her kitchen floor laid with marble tiles. Not that the floor really needed it. She thought that it might look prettier. Besides, she had to give him some work to get him to her house as often as possible. All the jobs that she had planned for him had been done, but she had got used to having him around. She wanted to see him more often, but the problem was that he did not have a mobile phone. There was no way she could contact him. She just had to wait for his call, which she did every minute of the day.

When he finally called, she was furious.

'Come here at once, there is a job to be done,' she said.

'What is it, ma'am?'

'Marble tiles have to be laid on the kitchen floor.'

'I wouldn't know how to do it, ma'am.'

'Neither do I, but you come and we'll give it a try,' she said.

He came and was shocked to see how she looked. She had dressed up as if she were going to a party. Her eyes twinkled like stars. She had made up her face, applied lipstick, groomed her hair and looked very attractive. As soon as she saw him, she laughed coyly and said, 'Ah! You are here! I have seen marble tiles being laid, not much skill is needed. I shall help you.' But he was still reeling from the effect her looks had on him.

Bending on her smooth knees, Amanda picked up the tiles one by one and gave them to him. He placed the tiles as she asked him to. He took the tile from her with his left hand and used the same hand to put the tile in place. 'So, you are a left-hander?' He nodded. If he made any mistake, she rapped him on his back. He liked that. A couple of errors even occurred deliberately. When they came to the centre of the floor, she handed him tiles with a beautiful floral design. After he had laid them, he moved his head left to right and right to left and admired his handiwork. She was ecstatic. 'You are a good worker,' she said and planted a kiss on his cheek. Work stopped halfway that day. They shared secrets, made plans and became lovers on the very same floor they had created minutes ago.

'What's that scar?' she touched his shoulder softly and asked him. 'While in combat, the enemy's bullet entered my shoulder and is lodged there permanently. The doctor said that it was dangerous to remove it and to let it be. So there it is.' Amanda kissed the scar. She pleaded with him to spend the night with her. But he said, 'No, ma'am, I am your servant.'

'Don't call me ma'am; call me Amanda.'

'Yes, ma'am,' he replied.

She arched her head back and blew into the nape of his neck, like one blows out the smoke of a cigarette. He wriggled in pleasure.

The refugee came during the day. Some days were also nights. He cooked dishes from his native land. They had dinners together. But one day in July, he who laughed easily and often did not laugh at all – he looked sad. When she asked him the reason, he hedged, saying this and that. But when Amanda pressed, he opened up. 'My lawyer says that from the 12th of June, Canada's new law has come into effect. It is bad for refugees. A refugee may be deported from this country even when his immigration case is under appeal. This scares me.'

She said, 'Canada's laws take their own time to come into effect. Before your number comes up for scrutiny, you will have become a citizen.'

'That's good news!'

He opened his mouth wide and laughed happily, voice full of hope. His eyes, as always, disappeared when he laughed. She laughed with him. He laughed again. As if a laughing contest was on between them, they kept laughing in turns.

Five friends of hers were coming for dinner. Amanda was not given to treating her friends to dinner all that frequently. But it was a time when she was floating in euphoria. She wanted to share her happiness with them. She busied herself in the kitchen from the early morning. She cooked fish curry the way her refugee lover had taught her. For the first time, she had used tamarind in the curry. Until she met him, she had not even been aware that such a condiment existed. She tasted the curry and found it had a wonderful amalgam of tastes.

She arranged six plates and napkins on the table. Then she stacked carefully the forks and knives. When she picked up her cell phone, attached to a charger, from the table, she found four voice messages – all from him. All were the same – a final goodbye.

'My lawyer says today is the day. I wanted to hear your voice one last time; but I have not been successful. Take a look in your mailbox. Goodbye,' said the voice. She could hear his voice crackling and sobbing. In the mailbox was an envelope with 500 dollars and a note inside. He had written in his 'not-so-perfect' English:

> They may come and arrest me today. They may deport me on the 7 o'clock flight. I am returning your 500 dollars. I don't know what will happen to me in my country. They may put me in jail and torture me. I could be branded a traitor and a deserter. Wherever I may be, I will spend every minute of what is left of my life thinking of you.
>
> With love,
> Arjuna Ranatunga

She moved her lips and rolled the name inside her mouth. He had told her that his name was chosen by his father in honour of a famous Sri Lankan left-handed cricketer. She turned her head this way and that, as if looking for her misplaced handbag. Her lungs refused to take in the air around her. She happened to see her own blurred reflection in the glass pane of the window. Her face and neck took on a colour quite different to the rest of her. Her breath came fast, shoving one over another. She stood there unmoving, waiting for the tremor in her hands to stop. She considered calling off the dinner party, but her guests had already begun to arrive one by one.

The dinner was over. The knives and forks were placed in the position of clock hands showing 8:20. Her friends were lavish in their praise of her fish curry. They pestered her for the recipe, and she promised to send it to them by email. Then they wanted to know where they could buy tamarind, and she told them. All she wanted to do was to speak to them of her refugee-lover. But the moment slipped away.

Her friends were amazed by the newly laid marble tiles in the kitchen. They stood there expressing their awe and appreciation. They said that the flower-patterned tile at the centre was what took the entire arrangement to a new level. Once again, she considered talking of her lover, but that moment went by too.

While she was changing into her night clothes, he came up in her thoughts again. Two Canadian armed guards from the border post would have handcuffed him and taken him to the plane as if he was a murderer. She remembered how he put his left hand around her waist. He used his left hand to strike with a hammer; he cut the fish with his left hand. He had said, 'I joined the army to earn a living. My enemy fought for a mission; giving up his life did not matter to him. But all I wanted was to save my life, and I committed the despicable act of taking refuge in a foreign country.'

Amanda could not sleep for a long time. Though lying in bed, she was in fact flying with him over the Atlantic. She cried aloud, 'Oh, my friends! I am, indeed, the sister of a witch. I know a refugee. He is the one who laid the tiles in my kitchen with his left hand; he is the creator of the fish curry as well; he is my secret lover. He is the one who walks around forever carrying a bullet buried in his left shoulder, a bullet from the gun of an enemy fighting to free his people.'

Then she laid down her head and drifted into peaceful sleep.

three

Son of a Chameleon!

T HEY CAUGHT HIM finally. It was two in the morning at the Petra border of Greece. The immigration corridor area where he stood was dilapidated and had caved in under the weight of all the millions of travellers who had stood there before him. In fact, standing there, he looked an inch shorter. Before this, he had been caught several times in different countries under different circumstances. But he'd never thought that he would be caught that day, because his passport and visa were so perfect. The chill pierced through his long overcoat and made him shiver. The border policeman narrowed his eyes and read the pages carefully as if he was examining an inscription on an ancient copper plate. A passport should have forty-eight pages, but his had only forty-six; it was something even he was not aware of, but they found that out.

When they took him into a small room, he felt he had

climbed into an elevator; it was the interrogation room. The officer behind the desk said, 'Tell me.' He asked, 'Tell what?' 'Tell me your story from the beginning,' said the officer. Even though he knew Greek, he pretended that he did not and started narrating his story in halting English.

'I took a job on a ship, three years ago, in 1983 in this very same country, Greece. The ship was called Argo. After my first trip to Brazil, I travelled to several countries. In fact, I went round the whole world. In the end, they sold the ship at Turkey's Bandirma port and I lost my job. When I was wondering what to do with my life, three Pakistanis helped me and that changed the course of my life. We stayed at a wonderful place in Turkey called Bosphorus, the place where the East and West meet. From our lodge, we could see the Blue Mosque.

'It was there that we decided to work for the Turkish Mafia. The mafia's strong network was like a parallel government. It was said that you could resolve any problem with their help. As I was yet a raw recruit, the Pakistanis showed me the ropes of the trade.

'In the 1980s, Turkey did not allow any import of cars. They were insanely expensive on the black market. Any car that met with an accident would immediately be stripped of its licence plates by the mafia. They would get a new, identical car from Switzerland and interchange the licence plates. Each car would be on offer for anything between $40,000 and $50,000. Our job was to fly to Switzerland and bring the particular brand of car that was in demand – drive it over to

Turkey. The job was a piece of cake. You set out from Zurich, drove through Italy, Yugoslavia and Bulgaria, and entered Turkey and got paid $5000. I have even smuggled two cars in a week. Those days we had so much money in our hands that we did not know how to spend it.

'One day, I saw the reflection of a girl on a marble floor in Switzerland and was enchanted by the image. Simona – that was her name – was a Swiss swimming champion and she had real blue eyes. If you looked into them deeply, you'd feel as if you were drowning in a sea. Whenever I happened to be in Switzerland, I stayed with her. Those were carefree days. Simona thought I was a rich trader. One day, I told her the truth and she jumped out of her seat. She was thrilled. She was a brave girl, always on the lookout for adventures. "Take me with you," she implored. The mafia would not approve of that and yet, I took her with me, and drove a new BMW for 2500 miles.

'As soon as we reached Turkey, I stopped at the first restaurant that we came across. At the entrance to the place, a man was playing on a wind instrument, holding it high in the air with both his hands. It physically changed as he played on it, becoming at times long and at other times short. I tipped him 100 lira. Simona snatched my wallet from me and dropped another 100 lira into his hand. That made her very happy. When we came back to our car after dinner, we found another car parked in front of ours. There was nobody in that car, but some noises came from inside it. Without a word to me, Simona just picked up a heavy spanner and gave the trunk of the car such a hard blow that it opened instantly. There was a huge man dumped in there, his hands and legs tied up. It was a wonder how they had squeezed such a huge body into that trunk. When we removed his gag, he pleaded with us to save him. As we didn't have time to think, we picked him up and sped away. Simona was overcome with joy, jumping like a dog with two tails.

'His name was Mehmet. He belonged to another group of gangsters and his enemies had caught him and were going to kill him. When we dropped him some twenty miles away, he thanked us with tears in his eyes and vowed that he would not forget our kindness. I handed over the car to my mafioso, got paid and spent the next four days in happiness with Simona. We stayed in the most expensive hotels. She photographed the Ayasofya a hundred times; that was a 1500-year-old building, initially a church, then a mosque, and now a museum. She asked me to stand in front of it for a photo. "Am I holding a gun to you, or am I a dentist, or an income-tax officer? Smile," she said. What is an income-tax officer? I asked. I didn't even know that such an official existed, or that one paid taxes on the money one earned.

'I cannot forget that night. Simona removed one shoe with another. It was funny the way she lay down between me and the wall. She always slept with both her legs folded in, looking like a crocodile. Suddenly, she came up with this question: "How is it that in all the paintings of Adam and Eve the leaves of the plant all appear to hide the same parts?" It was perhaps the result of having seen so many paintings in the museum earlier that day. I whispered the reason for that into her mouth. Her eyes shone in the dark. I kissed her on the nape of her neck where the colour of her hair changed. We didn't sleep at all that night and I never met her after that. She did not know that it was to be our last night together, nor did I.

'She raised her palm, as if taking an oath, at the divider in the airport and took leave of me. As the escalator steps went down one by one, the back of her head went out of my view. When I returned, two men followed me. They were Turkish policemen. They asked to see my passport. I realized immediately what it was all about. When you drove into Turkey, they stamped your passport with the image of a car. When you left the country with the car, the stamp would be removed. The police asked me, "Where is the car?" I was silent. I was put in prison; a prison with forty other inmates. I was in that hell for three days before the mafia came and bailed me out. I knew that the mafia wouldn't have much use for me in the future, now that the police knew of me. But they were decent people. They bought me a ticket to Qatar and arranged for a job on a ship there.

'Nineteen of us, including me, boarded the ship at Qatar. We introduced ourselves to each other. No one laughed when I told them my name, which was some comfort to me. There were no officers on that rather ancient and ghostly-looking ship. We spent the entire day confused about what we should do. At about 11 o'clock at night, a captain and two officers barged in. The ship did not carry any cargo; it did not have sufficient food supplies either. None of us knew what our destination was. We spoke to each other secretly and waited with trepidation in our hearts. We could feel that we were in great trouble.

'On the fourth day, the ship arrived at Djibouti and anchored for a day. No goods were loaded. When the ship crossed the Aden port after a few days, our fears grew. A Christian boy who worked with me began to cry. I told him, "Weeping does not need any special skill, even a baby can cry. This is the time we have to do what a sailor should do." He shivered and crossed himself. I asked him why he did that and he pointed to a spot and said, "This is where the grave of the first man on earth lies." I asked him if he meant Adam's grave. He said, "No! No! Adam was the first man created. But the one who died first was Abel, Adam's second son. Was he not murdered? You, too, make the sign of the cross and you will also be saved." I made the sign of the cross, thinking it could do me no harm anyway.

'The food supplies had run out a few days ago and, in fact, since the previous day, we'd had no water either. At 10 o'clock that night, the ship suddenly gained speed and began to shake terrifyingly. I knew the ship would not be able to handle that kind of speed. I tried to sit up and just when I thought nothing worse could happen, it did. The ship crashed with a loud noise on to a rock and slid down. There was a calendar on the wall with a Greek beauty's picture on it and, with the impact, the picture turned over and hung precariously at an odd angle. On the back of it was written this sentence in a child's scrawl: "Danger! They have planned to crash this ship and get the insurance money. Escape as soon as you can."

'When I hurried to the deck, men were trying to get away in lifeboats. I jumped in. They took us to Cairo, the capital city of Egypt, settled our wages, and packed us off with tickets to our various destinations. All the eighteen who were with me quietly accepted what was given to them and left. I understood their plan, which involved defrauding us of millions of dollars. When my turn came, they gave me an air ticket which was dated the 14th, though the accident had occured on the 17th of the month. I knew something was wrong. "This is just cheating us in the worst possible way. I will not let this pass without protest. I shall report you to the Lloyds Insurance Company. We should all be given proper compensation," I said. "We will take you to our superior," they said.

'After two days, they made me go through the alleys of Cairo and took me to the basement of an old building. Inside it was bright and well furnished. Two armed guards stood there, holding on tightly to their guns. Their chief was reclining on a throne-like seat, half of him spilling out of the seat. He had a sarong around his waist and no shirt. Folds of his belly rested on each other. He turned his face towards me. Involuntarily, a scream escaped from my throat. "Mehmet!" It was him! The same man who had been left folded and tied up inside the boot of a car! With great difficulty, he ran to me, crying, "My friend!" and gave me a big hug, and I disappeared into him. He said, "I have been ordered to kill you. You saved me once, now it is my turn. Let our accounts be settled. If you are caught one more time, I will kill you. Ask me what you want and I shall give it to you."

'I could have asked for an American visa or a French visa. I could have even asked to be sent to Simona's country. Instead, I asked to be sent to Greece. It was Mehmet who sent me to this place, with enough money for the passage,' the immigrant finished his narration.

Both border guards looked at each other, listening to this unbelievable story. One of them asked him, 'Why did you want to come back here?'

'It was here that I began my career,' the immigrant said. Now a third man, who looked like their superior, entered the room. He surveyed the man in their custody as though he was looking at a strange animal. 'This son of a chameleon! What story is he giving you?' he said. 'The whole night he has been telling us an impossible tale,' they told their superior.

The three of them put their heads together and gave the issue some consideration; they argued loudly. They could put him in prison, but that would mean expenditure. They could send him back, but that would also mean that the government would have to shell out money for his ticket. In fact, that would be even more of a loss. The officer held the forty-six-page passport in his hand and waving it, said in Greek, 'He must be rich. Why don't we kill him?' Those pitiful descendants of great Greek minds like Pythagoras, Plato, Archimedes and other prodigious men of that country seemed to think through their tiny brains. They debated on and on. He felt like laughing. It was now exactly three years, four months and eight days since he had left Sri Lanka. No punishment that these little men could come up with would ever equal all that he had already suffered. Any decision that they might arrive at was acceptable to him. Pitiable souls! They had only one country to call their own. But all the countries in the entire world were his.

four

Rat Face

THE NEWLY ENFORCED LAW was the hot topic of the day. People gathered in groups to talk about it: 'This is a basic right of the human race,' said a girl student who was all of ten years old. 'How dare the government interfere in this! No other country in the world has any such law. America's reputation as a pioneer in progressive reforms seems to be a thing of the past. It is clearly falling behind the times. We must fight for our rights.'

'I will write about it on my website,' a boy proclaimed.

'Aha! Do that, and they will honour you by naming a street after you,' someone said and everyone laughed.

Finally it was decided that news of this infamous law should be spread worldwide through the miphone and other communications. The US government might surely see some sense then.

Samantha, however, was not really worried about any of

this. There were only five more days for the year 2029 to come to a close, and that was when she would begin her twelfth year. On that day her life would undergo a major change. This law wouldn't be able to touch her then.

The law was not all that bad to begin with. All it did was to stipulate that a person should not change sex more than three times in his or her lifetime. That was all. Samantha had two mothers. Of those two, the one who had not given birth to her had initially been male. That was how, and when, Samantha was conceived. He then became female, and Samantha ended up having two mothers. The mother who had borne her in her womb had promised her that she would change into a male on the last day of that year, 2029. Tired of dealing with two mothers, Samantha was looking forward to 2030, when she would have a father and a mother. She quietly chanted the word, Papa, many times to herself.

Samantha sat next to Marty in the classroom. She spent all her waking hours talking to Marty over the miphone. Marty was a very beautiful girl; she wore dresses that changed colours on their own according to the time of the day. Samantha was not as beautiful as Marty; she had a slightly protruding face. Her face sort of preceded her when she entered a room.

Marty had pictures of her father and mother as wallpaper on her miphone screen. Marty's father had been male before his marriage. Since he longed to carry a baby in his body, he changed his sex, conceived a baby, and became a man once again after Marty was born. Marty's mom was a mother only

29

in name. She had never been interested in getting pregnant or delivering a baby.

Samantha's teacher, Roberto, was a different case altogether. It was said that he had once had a robot for a lover. He would say, 'Everyone in this world should change sex at least once in his or her lifetime, only then will they be able to really understand the opposite sex. The emotions of both the sexes are contradictory. So the only way to get a fuller understanding of the ways of the world is to see it by – at one time or another – being both sexes.' True to his declaration, one day he suddenly changed into a woman and came to the class. When he walked, the blue dress he wore moved as if it had a life of its own. He told them his name was now Rebecca. How beautiful he looked! His slim waist, his hair, broad shoulders, and the fluttering of his eyes made him the envy of all the girl students. When there was a poll in the class as to which sex he should be, twenty-four of the thirty students in the class voted that he should remain a female.

Samantha would have been happy if she could have gone to school five days a week. Her real mother said that was how it was during her own school days. But now they had to attend school only three days a week and spend the other two work days studying at home. Teachers conducted classes on the internet. Questions were asked, tests held, all on the internet. She felt it wasn't any fun. She would keep sending her teacher text messages enquiring about her marks, and the reply would come, but no instant appreciation or applause could be expected. That would come much later.

Mama had a lot to say about the days when she was younger. People back then had to wait until they were sixteen to get their driving licence. Now you could get one when you were just twelve, and cars did not have to be driven manually. If you gave it the destination, it took you there. On the very first day of 2030, she would get a Sun-car. Many of her friends owned Sun-cars. Fuel was no longer a pressing issue and the environment was not being polluted any more.

Samantha was looking forward to the day her school would reopen, but in the meantime, she was kept busy by something nasty that was being broadcast about her on miphones all over the world. Samantha saw it by chance and was shocked.

She had an enemy in her class. The boy had two mothers and a father, and that was a matter of pride to him. His name was Noah, and in utter contrast to the biblical Noah who saved creatures by ferrying them in his Ark after the great deluge, this Noah took great pleasure in tormenting people. He always came first in Math. When they took the test at the regional level, however, Samantha knew what happened to the time period when the length of the pendulum was cut short, but he didn't. That did it, and much to her own surprise, she topped the list in that exam, and Noah came second. She knew that boys made fun of her behind her back, mocking her long face. The message Noah had sent on the miphone was this: 'A rat might win a race, but a rat will always be a rat.' It hurt her so much, she felt a burning sensation in all her bones. She wanted to fall into Marty's arms and have a good cry.

Even before the year 2030 set in, the headmaster had sent his opening-day address on the miphone. She liked half of what he had said. 'If you sit on a bicycle, you have to keep moving. Or else you will fall down. Your job is to keep moving. The earth rotates towards the east – this is not knowledge, it is just a simple fact. There is no use in knowing only this. Enquiring what would happen if the earth started rotating westwards is the mark of progress towards knowledge. May your bicycles keep moving!'

Samantha liked the speech up to this point. What she did not like was that he had claimed that when a door closed, another would open. This was something that had been said since the 18th century. But no one ever told you that the second door opened on the 37th floor; nor did they tell you that the elevator didn't work. Mama said, 'It is not enough if you are clever; hard work in equal proportion is also necessary.' 'But the earthworm seems to work hard, too – only to go into the hen's mouth,' she thought.

Yesterday, Samantha had watched her mother's favourite movie, Titanic, on the home screen with her. How childish the movie was! The famous red dress Kate Winslet wore made Samantha want to laugh out loud. A weaverbird would have perhaps made a better dress. Real men and women acted in that film. The story was something a six-year-old could have written. Nothing like present-day stories, in which it was so difficult to predict how things began and how they ended, sustaining the element of suspense throughout. Often, a second viewing of the same movie would appear quite changed with new endings thrown in. And there were no real persons acting. All movies were shot on low budgets from a small room using digital technology.

There were many interesting students at Samantha's school. Annette was a classmate of hers whom she was very fond of. The girl was forever in tears, and she also had a half-eaten sandwich in her hand all the time. She was Dutch. She did not know a word of English. She read her books in Dutch, gave her answers in Dutch, wrote her tests in Dutch, and the miphone translated all that instantly into English. The girl from Iceland was wonderstruck at everything she saw around her. She even looked at the sun every day with wonder. The student from Portugal forgot his own mother's name one day. The students spoke different languages, but the miphone made learning a new language completely unnecessary. The result was that teachers of French, Spanish, Latin and Greek were declared redundant, and they lost their jobs.

Just as it had been promised, she got a father on the new year's day of 2030. He even had a moustache! Samantha hugged and kissed him in delight, and she saved the photo of her father and mother taken together as the wallpaper on the screen of her miphone. When she went to school that day, she did not carry books, pencils, pens or paper. All she had to have with her was a miphone. At the entrance to her house, a two-seater Sun-car was waiting for her. Even as she approached it, it opened its door to her, and locked itself as soon as she got in. Though it had snowed the previous night, the inside of the car was warm and nice. She only had to say, 'School,' and the car started on its own. Thousands of cars chased each other on the road. Two-seaters, four-seaters, six-seaters, all of them running on solar power. There were no speed limits, and no accidents either. So no seat belts, no air bags, not even traffic lights. But the cars stopped now and then, as if obeying some unheard command, and let other cars pass by.

Halfway through, Samantha seemed to have a change of mind and she simply said, 'Madera coffee house.' She did not specify any particular coffee house, but the car chose the one nearest to them. Research claimed that Madera coffee sharpened one's brain. Some five hundred years ago, an Ethiopian shepherd boy had seen his goats eat the seeds of a particular plant and jump and frolic. He plucked some of them, brewed them in hot water and drank the decoction. He began to jump with joy as well. Madera coffee was being prepared following the same ancient procedure. A medical team had certified that the brew indeed raised one's spirits.

Samantha stood near the first counter and said, 'Junior coffee, superior.' At the next counter the coffee arrived in a paper cup. She took the cup and merely said, 'Thank you.' The sound of her voice would transfer the required money from her account to the coffee shop's account. Credit cards had disappeared even during her mother's days. Currency had long gone out of circulation. The only money she had ever seen was a 20 dollar bill with the picture of Andrew Jackson on it, which Marty treasured. Now most things were done through the miphone. Samantha's had registered the lines on her palm, her eyes, voice, double-stranded DNA and so on. No one else could use that phone. It could be operated only by her voice, the lines on her palm or her eyes.

When Samantha reached her school, the car stopped at a predetermined place. After she got out, the car door closed on its own. She commanded, 'Go to the parking lot,' and left. She met headmaster Jones on her way to class. He was wearing a long black overcoat. She greeted him. He returned her greeting, smiling. She said, 'That was an excellent introductory address.' He thanked her and moved away, his red hair flapping. His hair had been green the previous week. He would be seventy-five in another couple of months and would retire. He was a good man. He had been saying that he wanted to be a woman when he retired. Many had asked him, 'Why a female?' 'Loneliness and ageing are best handled by women. Men are not smart enough to deal with them. Nor do they have the patience,' he had replied. But, unfortunately, he would not be allowed to fulfil his desire. He had already changed his sex three times. According to the new law, he'd have to manage the rest of his life as a male.

It was with some hesitation that she walked into her class that day. She felt her stomach clenched in fear. Noah would be there. He had spoiled her expectations of having a fine first day. She stood near the door of her class. The clock on the door showed that there was exactly one minute for the class to begin. She did not know then there was something waiting to happen inside the class to make her bad beginning even worse. The door read the lines of her eyes, registered her identity and opened. She entered the class and the door closed behind her.

All the other seats in the class had already been taken. She walked to her seat, but she froze. She saw a boy sitting in Marty's seat. She said, 'Who are you? Why are you sitting here? This is Marty's seat.' The whole class laughed out loud. Her face grew long and red, looking a lot like a rat's face. The boy said, 'Don't call me Marty. I am Martin now.' Samantha stared in disbelief. 'You cheat! We were such good friends, and you didn't tell me your plan. And here I am, coming so eagerly to show you a picture that I had taken of my parents. I am a fool! I am a fool!' she shouted and threw her miphone fiercely at the wall. It hit the wall and shattered into a thousand pieces. Then, the pieces, of their own accord, came together again. And even as she watched, it started moving towards her.

five

The Good Earth

B ARELY FOUR DAYS after arriving in Canada, Seelan asked his mother, 'Do you have a gun?'

'Certainly not! What kind of a question is that?'

'They say America has more guns than people. Is that true?'

'But this is not America; this is Canada.'

'Do our neighbours have a gun?'

'Now, now! Do you plan to go to our neighbours and borrow their gun, just like you borrowed their ladder? Jesus! What is happening here!'

'Don't you worry, Mama. I was just thinking of how best we could protect ourselves.'

'We have no enemies here. You are free to go around anywhere you want. This is a peaceful country.'

'I have carried a gun on me for over twenty years. It feels strange to be without one.'

'Don't even think about it. A hammer in the hand will make you see nails everywhere.'

That conversation did not go well. Any chat with him grew serious and went in completely unanticipated directions.

As a young lad, Seelan had been a good student. But one day he left for school and never came home. It was rumoured that he had joined the movement. After a long wait, his family gave up any hope of his return and migrated to Canada. Once there, his father got into the business of producing plastic spare parts and succeeded quite remarkably in his venture. After the war ended in Sri Lanka, he spent a fortune searching for his son, found him in a camp, and brought him back to Canada via Thailand.

Seelan was flabbergasted at the sight of his parents' house in Canada. It could be called a mansion, built as it was on half an acre of land. Marble floors, ornamental woodwork, spiral staircases, curtains that could be opened and closed by a remote control, a television that was wider than the distance between it and the viewers. Such a lavish lifestyle had never ever been part of his dreams. 'Such a big house!' he said. He was confused. Whom had he fought the war for? Had it not been for them as well? But it looked like they had forgotten their country; they had forgotten that a war had been fought to claim their land. 'You never thought of me, ever,' he said.

'Dear son! Was there ever a day when we did not think of you or pine for you? We chose to live here, live this kind of life, just so you could be happy when you finally got here. You must build a good life for yourself.'

'How can I ever do that? I am unable to forget the past.'

'It's been five years since we moved into this house. Letters to the previous owner keep coming in even now. Likewise, old memories have a way of trailing us. You should learn to ignore them and embrace this new life.'

'How do I do that? Do you know how much I have lost? While I was there, at war, a new country, Kosovo, was born. I was not even aware of that. If somebody said the time of the day was 23:20, I would not know what it meant. If it was 4 o'clock there, what time would it be in other parts of the world? I had no idea. Yesterday, you quoted a beautiful line from a poem: "A butterfly is hauling a forest on its legs." Who can say what forest I carry on my legs? After fighting for a land for more than twenty years, all that I have now are two old shirts, a pair of old slippers, a broken wrist watch, and new enemies…' His mother said, 'What enemies? You have no enemies here. Two hundred people work in your father's factory. You should learn the job from your father. Also, we shall look for a good bride for you.'

It was like any other day, a day just like the day before, and perhaps not very different from how the next day might turn out. His mother fried prawns, made a dish of dried fish and cooked some yellow rice. He wanted to cry as he ate. Mama's food had not changed a wee bit even after all those years. His palate still remembered it. Once a Sri Lankan army helicopter had flown into their area and dropped packets of food for the army. One of those packets came drifting, carried by the strong wind to them. It contained yellow rice and

39

meat. The freedom fighters were always hungry and he and his friends fell over each other for their share of the parcel and ate it hungrily. Not one of those friends was alive today.

That night he exhaled on the window and scribbled the letters 'Manjula' in the condensation. As soon as he wrote her name, it began to disappear. She was the girl who had come into his life and to whom he had looked up in awe all the time. When he had first met her, she was one year, two months and fourteen days away from the day of her death. All the words they had exchanged put together would not have exceeded a hundred. But she spoke eloquently with her wide eyes. Pradeep, the master who trained her, used to say that he had never seen in his career a warrior like her. She was slender, but she could walk a couple of miles with a fifty-kilo load on her back. Her full-time job was to make fun of Seelan's skills with his rifle. 'You seem to shoot first and then take aim!'

She was thorough with the code words of their movement. 'Coconut' meant 'death while fighting'; 'tender coconut' was 'hurt while fighting'; 'throw' was 'food'. She had coined some code words on her own to refer to him. 'Palm fruit' meant 'I love you'; 'palai' stood for 'I cannot bear to be away from you'; and 'frond' for 'come at once'. That girl, who had so loved him, enrolled herself into the suicide squad one day without even a word to him. Just before they left on an attack, she removed her wristwatch and gave it to him. He thought that it had stopped working and she wanted him to set it right. Only the previous day Seelan had told her, 'As I get closer to you, I seem to find more new dimensions to you. I don't think there will ever be an end to this. I don't think there could be a last page to our story.'

'Last page? I am writing it tomorrow,' she had replied. He did not understand the import of her words then. It was only later that he realized that she had given him the watch as a memento. He had brought it with him to Canada.

He was captured in the Mullivaikkal round-up. He was locked up with fifty thousand or more in the Arunachalam open prison in Chettikulam. It had high, barbed wire fences and two tiers of security. There was no way to escape.

Every morning as he woke up, he would marvel, 'Oh! I am not dead yet!' Every day, he was dragged in front of one of the officers for questioning. Just as Jesus had been nailed to the cross as soon as Pontius Pilate had washed his hands of him and signalled to his men, a mere shake of that officer's head could be the cue for a bullet to enter his chest. The officer asked questions but did not maintain any written record of the answers Seelan gave him. Nothing was tape-recorded either. It was like they were playing a game. Every day, it was a new officer asking questions, and the interrogation was interspersed with punches in the face or blows with a club. The questions never varied, nor did the answers. The only difference was each day a new officer whipped him. By the time he prepared himself to answer one set of questions, another volley of four would have been shot at him already.

'In the movement you were known by the name Selvakumar?'

'I was never in the movement, sir.'

'Is it not you in this photo, the one with the short beard and small moustache?'

'That is a different Seelan, sir.'

'Who is this, in this picture, wearing dark glasses?'

'Another Seelan, sir.'

'In the war at Mankulam, the one who threw a bomb and captured the army bunker, was that not you? Your name was in all the papers?'

'That too was another Seelan.'

That was when the officer kicked him. He was thrown back four feet, along with the chair he was sitting on. He lost consciousness. When he came to, he was in the hospital.

Mankulam was his first place of combat. That was where he wore the uniform and actively participated in fighting after three months of physical training and another three months of learning how to wield weapons. Their squad had fifteen soldiers, all new to the conflict. When they reached their target, gunfire confronted them from an underground bunker. They had not expected this and within ten seconds into the war, fourteen of his comrades had died. He was the only one lying alive and unwounded deep inside a pit. His heart was beating fast. He flung the grenade he held in his hand. By fluke, it went straight into the bunker and after that there was no more firing. He jumped into the bunker and took cover. Outside, fierce fighting continued and he spent the next twenty-four hours with two dead bodies beside him. That's how he became part of the history of Mankulam.

As he settled into his new life in Canada, Mama began to talk to him about a certain girl. Marriage? At his age? He was almost forty years old and his conscience would not accept it. When the girl visited their house, Mama introduced her. She smiled in a condescending way, the way a mistress smiles at a servant. Above her wax-white legs, she wore a flared skirt and walked with quick, short steps on high heels. She did not know that he was an ex-freedom fighter, but he was forever conscious of his war tally: seven killings, two prisons, four training camps, three full-fledged combats, two minor ones, seven scars, the capture of a bunker, and a love affair. Rearranging her hair once every fifteen minutes, touching up her lips once every thirty minutes, and shaping her eyebrows every ten minutes…what chance did he have with this girl?

In the jungles, before and after he washed his face, before and after he had his meals, unfastening and fastening the gun at his waist, he had only one thought: 'How were they to create a nation? How were they to make a land of their own?' For twenty years, that had been his way of life.

'Where you live is your country. Where you have rights, there your land is; that is inside you and nobody can take it away from you. You are a good boy. Your character cannot be determined by the number of people you have killed. Only by the way you showed kindness to those you did not kill,' his mother said.

One person in his group of fighters was adept at seizing weapons. Dhananjayan had eleven weapons to his credit in the Elephant Pass combat led by Paulraj Anna, and that was quite a record. In the war of the epic Mahabharata, when Uttamakumaran set out to fight, his sister, Utharai, would ask him to bring back silk stoles, jewellery and crowns from the enemy. In a similar fashion, the fighters now placed their requests for firearms. 'I want an M70, Anna!' 'AK 47 for me,' 'RI 56 is what I want!' would be the various demands assailing Dhananjayan. Some greedy men asked even for AK LMGs. Dhananjayan somehow always succeeded in stripping his dead enemies of all and any kind of weapons. But on the third day of war, as soon as the opponent fell down hit by a bullet, Dhananjayan ran towards the falling body. Like a flash, he removed the gun from the wounded soldier and was halfway back to his men, when a bullet pierced his back. He fell on his face but still did not lose his hold on the captured gun. Seelan carried the wounded friend on his back and ran to safety. Bullets hissed from close quarters and flames lit up all around them. The blood that flowed from his friend's chest dripped down Seelan's back and on to his feet. Seelan ran a mile before he realized his friend was dead.

As far as his father was concerned, he believed his duty was over once Seelan got to Canada. He would walk before Seelan like a hotel waiter, his hands locked behind his back. He expected his son to join him in the factory and assist him. But Seelan wouldn't even discuss it. Very often, he walked out of the house not even bothering to shut the door behind him. One day, his mother came looking for him and found him sitting under a tree, staring vacantly at the sky. 'What are you looking at, son?'

'Mama! I am listening to the sounds of April.'

'Oh, Jesus! Does April make sounds? Come inside, son. It is chilly out there.'

'Then is it not the month of April now?'

'Don't talk like a fool!'

'A couple of fools more in this world is not going to make things worse,' he said.

His mother once asked him, 'What did you do on your days off?'

He could not bear that question. It shocked him that she could even ask. His own mother was unaware that fighters did not take days off. His group had to hide in a jungle for ten days before they could launch a surprise attack. During the attack, all the food and water that they had brought with them ran out. For two whole days they went without food or water, but they carried out their mission at the appropriate time and returned to their camp. During those tense moments, not one of them had complained of hunger or thirst or suggested that they turn back. That was how dedicated they were. And his mother probably spent those very hours debating what colour she should choose to get her kitchen painted! He was ashamed of his parents. Every minute he spent in their house was hell for him.

Before she went to bed, his mother always locked the front door and hid the key. Yet, one morning, she entered his room and found his bed, white sheets tucked in, empty. One of the windows was open. It was snowing outside and he was gone. There was no clue as to when in the night he could have left home. Unfamiliar with the place as he was, he lost his way very often. The weatherman announced there would be four inches of snow on that day. The police were informed at once and announcements were made in the newspapers and on television. His body was found after a week, one mile away in a ravine. Covered with snow, Seelan's face looked as if he was smiling.

Seelan's father had bought three plots of land in the Resthaven Memorial Gardens, a cemetery in Toronto, at a premium price. It is here he hoped they would all be buried. All three spots were side by side. Even in that bitter cold, a dozen people showed up for the funeral. The priest said his prayers: 'Our Lord, our Father, just as the servant's eyes are always turned towards the hands of his master, our eyes are always turned towards you until you show us mercy. Bless him wholly on this day so that the soul you created comes back to you. Amen.'

Seelan's snow-covered body, which was born in Mayiliddi, Yazhppanam and which escaped Mullivaikkal and reached here via Thailand, was now laid to rest in Toronto. He finally had a piece of land that truly belonged to him. Now, no one could ever take it away from him.

six

Gravity Tax

HIS HANDS SHOOK even as he opened the letter. He knew where it had come from. He had not paid the gravity tax for the past three months. This was the third and final reminder directing him to pay it without delay. This annoyance had been on for two years. Before that, there hadn't been such a disastrous concept as the Gravitation Department and its tax.

'Madam!'

'How may I help you?'

'I have received another reminder about the overdue gravity tax.'

'May I know who is speaking?'

'I am speaking from 14, Lawrence Street.'

'And your issue is?'

'The bill is very high; can you review it once more, please?'

'I have just opened your account. I remember speaking

47

with you last month as well, and you made the same request then, too. You used to be so regular with paying your bills. What's wrong now?'

'My financial situation has worsened.'

'What can we do about that? We have calculated your charges precisely according to the handout we sent out earlier; the one listing the rules and regulations of the department.'

'Your handout is very bulky. The letters are so tiny that they run away like crawling ants even before I finish reading them. Nor am I able to understand the basis of your tax calculations. They seem very unfair.'

'How can your inability to understand them make them unfair? You pay a tax for water, you pay the electricity bill, the gas bill, solar tax, pure air tax, and so on and so forth. You also settle your television and telephone bills in no time. Why is this unfair?'

'Madam! What connection do I have with the earth's gravity? That has been in existence all the time. It was here even before Sir Isaac Newton discovered it. No tax was ever levied on gravity all these years. How can you begin to extract a fee for using it now for just these past two years?'

'Sir, what you say is surprising! Why did you not think of raising this question two years earlier? We bring water to your house. We purify the air and give it to you to breathe. We let your gadgets operate with the help of the sunlight that falls on your roof. We provide gas and electricity. And you pay all the bills that we charge but oppose just this one bill, the earth's gravity bill. Just give it a thought. Can you live even for a minute if the earth exerted no force of gravity at all? Would you be able to drive your car? Or walk? Could your children run around and play? Without gravity, you can't do even such an insignificant act as passing urine!'

'Madam! My mouse-brain refuses to comprehend these arguments. But what does your department do in this matter? Does it have to clean up the earth's gravity or convey it to our house? Don't you think it is gross injustice to make us pay for some service that is not rendered by your department?'

'All the people of the United States pay this tax. European countries have established this tax. Even some African nations have introduced it. The world is progressing phenomenally, and here you are behaving in such an unpatriotic manner. It is sad that you know the importance of earth's gravity, you use it fully and yet you hesitate to pay a charge for it. I may have to complain about you to the higher authorities.'

'Madam, how can your sweet voice even utter the word "complain"? Have I not been very regular in my payments ever since this department began functioning? I have great love for my country, for this earth and for its gravity as well. I never go to bed without reading at least one poem on earth's gravity. I shall try somehow to settle your bill, please bear with me. Good day!'

'Good day!'

'Hello!'

'Hello!'

'Is that 14, Lawrence Street? Is it the resident of the house speaking?'

'Yes, it is. Please tell me what I can do for you?'

'Sir! I am calling from the Department of Gravitation. You have been using our services without paying the bills for the past four months. I am sorry to inform you that the time to take action against you is close at hand.'

'Madam! What kind of tactic is this? I have deep financial constraints. Please, have some mercy on me. I have not refused to pay the tax. I just need some more time. I shall somehow pay my dues before the earth's gravity comes to an end.'

'You think this is smart talk. You have been allowed eight grace periods until now. According to the standards we have set for our functioning, you are a cheat. If you do not settle your dues immediately, you will have to face very severe consequences.'

'Madam, should you be using such harsh words? I am not capable of even spelling the word "cheat" correctly; I am not that kind of person either. Somebody has, perhaps, told you that in my younger days, I stole and sold my mother's chicken without her knowledge. Your voice is like divine music to my ears. Should you be uttering such unkind words to me? I shall settle the entire bill before the end of this month.'

'Right. Do that. Just make sure that our department does not have to contact you over this again.'

'Absolutely! But I do need to clear just one doubt. Your charges seem to be increasing every month. Why is it so?'

'Did you not read our circular no. 148.8?'

'No, madam.'

'Read page 48 of that circular. You use the earth's gravity.

Your wife uses it. Your two children as well. Isn't your weight going up every month? That means you are consuming more of earth's gravity every month. If only you had asked your eight-year-old son, he would have given you the right answer.'

'How is it that you know my son is eight years old? All of this just seems so ridiculous!'

'Sir! We know everything about you. We know that your son was born in Albert Martin hospital, and that he weighed 7 pounds 8 ounces at birth. Have you noticed that your wife's girth is expanding rapidly?'

'You exceed your limits, madam.'

'You asked me why the charges were going up, and I just gave the reasons for that. There are many who have benefited by this scheme. Do you know that some of them have brought down their weight considerably?'

'Madam! How do you know precisely how much we weigh?'

'You should have read circular no. 133.6. As of today, your weight is 174 pounds. Last month it was 172. The magic eyes installed in your houses send us all these data.'

'Madam, we were not in this country for the past couple of weeks. We were travelling abroad. Don't we get any discount for that? We did not, then, use the earth's gravity of this country, right?'

'Sir, our department considered all these issues very deeply long before our rules were formulated. Prepare an affidavit stating, "We were not using this country's gravity from such and such a date" and send it to us through your lawyer; we shall credit the amount to your account.'

'Thank you, madam, thank you. What an exemplary system! Even though the sharpness of your intellect pierces my heart, the sweetness in your voice throws me off balance. Would you permit me to ask just one more question?'

'Okay. Ask away.'

'My mother-in-law is bedridden. She sleeps on a cot, her dentures sleep inside a glass by her side. She never uses earth's gravity. Does she get any concession for that?'

'That you should ask me such a question! You should be really ashamed of yourself. Let us assume your mother-in-law does not use earth's gravity; in that case, how could she be lying down on the cot? Would she not be flying past the planet Uranus by now?'

'I am really sorry! You have really sharpened my intellect. I promise you, I'll pay the Earth Gravity charges immediately.'

'Just do that first!'

'Hello!'

'Hello!'

'Sir! Your promise seems to be flying past the planet of Uranus. I am sorry to give you the final warning. You have to pay all the outstanding dues within a week.'

'Madam! How can you be so harsh? Do I have the resources and yet refuse to pay what I owe you? I have paid the air tax; I have paid the gas tax and the water tax, as also the entertainment tax.'

'That is exactly what puzzles me. You pay all the taxes

that the various departments levy, but you hesitate to pay the Earth Gravity tax.'

'Don't you know the reason for that?'

'No, I don't; please explain it to me.'

'If I do not pay the electricity dues, my power connection will be cut off. Water supply will be stopped if I do not pay the charges for it; air, telephone, gas will all be cut off similarly. But if I don't pay the Earth Gravity tax, can you sever it? Even a resurrected Newton will not be able to do that.'

'Sir! If you, who cannot read a circular, could come up with such brilliant reasoning, just think how deeply the scientists of this department would have analysed all possible issues. Did you read the newspaper last week?'

'Madam, you ask questions much like my former fourth grade teacher.'

'Sir, it is clear that you do not go through our circulars; I accept that. But what's wrong with the newspapers? Why and how have they offended you?'

'Madam, when I read newspapers, evil spirits torment me in my dreams. What am I to do?'

'Right then. Wait for the evil spirits to go away and then go back to reading the newspaper. Perhaps then you would stay abreast of things.'

'Madam! Please do alleviate my curiosity. I cannot bear it. Just be kind enough to tell me what was in the papers.'

'I shall, indeed, tell you. One person was cheating the Earth Gravity Department, withholding the charges for eight full months.'

'Is that so?'

'We levied a fine, but he did not pay that either. So then we decided that he should not use the earth's gravity any more.'

'What happened after that?'

'We carted him in a space rocket and discharged him to a place where there was no gravity. He went around the earth just once before he had a change of mind and agreed to pay our taxes. We then brought him back to earth.'

'Is that true? What a wonderful scheme!'

'The man paid all the money that he owed us, including the fines. He even paid the interest on the sum. But he is still in trouble.'

'Oh, why would that be?'

'He now pays, in monthly instalments, the cost of his travel in the space rocket, his space outfit and other expenses incurred by our department. He will pay off the entire amount in 2196 months.'

'2196 months?!'

'Oh, yes! It will take him 183 years to pay it all off.'

'Will he live that long?'

'We do not know about that. His heirs will have to take on the responsibility of settling their father's debts.'

'Madam! I will remit all that I owe you, immediately, to the last cent.'

'Hello!'
　'Hello!'

'The people from the Earth Gravity Department have nothing but praise for you. They said that you were very prompt in paying all your taxes.'

'Thank you. May I know who is speaking? Your voice sounds a little like the croaking of a strangled duck.'

'I am speaking from the department of Earth Travels.'

'Is this a new department?'

'What? You do not know of it? Did you not get our circular? Your charges are in arrears for the past three months.'

'What dues are you talking about?'

'The earth's travel fees. You know the planet earth goes round the sun. In one revolution, you travel 149,600,000 kilometres. Just imagine! You travel all that distance for free! Not a cent do you spend on that trip. But you will not get the facility free any more. You have to pay for the trips you make.'

'Right! What a scintillating idea! From now on, we will stop counting the days and start keeping the account in kilometres! The very thought thrills me!'

'Send us the charge for the first three months. You can then thrill about it. The distance you have travelled so far is 37,400,000 kilometres.'

'Don't you worry! I shall write a cheque singing merrily, sign it and send it to you. But just one question. Just as it is for air travel, are there different classes of travel – first, second and third classes?'

'No, not at all!'

'Very good! I am very much in favour of this. So is my mother.'

55

'You have a concession as well.'

'Is that so? Tell me!'

'The leap year has a day more, right? But we do not charge extra money for that. You pay the same amount.'

'Unbelievable! You deserve a pearl necklace for giving me this dazzling news. Or perhaps, at least a red apple that has no black dots. It is, indeed, news that thrills one. Can you not charge the rich some extra?'

'Look how intelligently you are able to think now. This earth needs more people like you. You have to pay extra if you carry excess baggage when you fly. The same rule applies here.'

'For example?'

'If a rich man has four houses, five cars and plenty of other things, he has to pay excess fare. Ordinary people do not have to pay anything extra.'

'Madam! I do not have words to laud you. I shall send my travel fees today.'

'Good! What was that sound?'

'Nothing. That was the sound of earth turning a corner.'

'While talking to me these past ten minutes, you have travelled 18,000 kilometres. Do please include the charges for that as well when you make your payment.'

'Most certainly! What could give me more pleasure than settling your bill? Another thing…'

'What is it?'

'I had planned a holiday and now that I am on this trip around the universe, why bother about minor tours? So I have decided to cancel that. I will save on that expense and arrange to pay your earth travel tax at once.'

'You are one great earth enthusiast.'

'Madam! I have a suggestion. The stars are twinkling all the time, no one pays any tax for that. The moon waxes and wanes over and over again. Something has to be done to make use of all that to generate income. Nobody seems to be bothered about it.'

'Excellent idea! We shall definitely look into that.'

seven

Bodyguard

IT HAPPENED AT exactly 4 o'clock in the afternoon on an ordinary day. I remember the precise time because at that very moment, the tower clock behind the bus stop rang resoundingly. The bus stop was across the road from where I stood. My eyes looked up at the clock and then slid down. What happened then changed my entire life.

My sister-in-law, Machal, always began to worry just as the clock struck three in the afternoon. My elder brother, whom I called Annar, returned home from his office every day exactly at 5:30 p.m. His office closed at 5 p.m. I can imagine his routine at the end of the workday: he closes the files for the day when the clock strikes five, puts the cap on his pen and clips it on to his shirt pocket, locks the drawer, and after safely depositing the key in a secure place, goes and stands at the bus stop in front of his office. How else would he manage to be home exactly at 5:30 p.m. every day?

Annar expected his dinner, all of a boiled egg, to be ready as soon as he stepped into the front yard of the house. It was about this that my Machal was perpetually worried. She'd bustle around as if the Sri Lankan Parliament would collapse if she could not get the egg ready in time. At ten minutes to four, Machal would give me some money and ask me to go get an egg. It should be a red egg; my brother never ate the white ones. How could a person who held the post of a head clerk in a government office be expected to eat white eggs? I had, on many occasions, asked her why it was that we did not buy a dozen eggs at a time and stock them. Such questions made her angry. Her eyes would get bigger and bigger and become the size of the red eggs I bought daily. 'Does a hen ever lay a dozen eggs in a day? It lays only one,' she would say. What kind of an answer was that? But Machal's word was the law. If I protested, the matter would be reported to Annar. I had to remind myself of my status in that house – I was a slave.

After the second time I failed my examinations to get into university, they decided that a polytechnic course was my only option and enrolled me. Annar was paying my fees, he was feeding me, and he was giving me a place to stay. Every year, he bought me a new shirt and gave me an old one he no longer wanted. I would be seventeen in another two months.

What was wrong with fattening one's own Annar by getting him an egg at exactly four every afternoon? I entered the egg shop, tossing the coin I had in my hand. It was then that the clock struck four and I saw her standing at the bus stop. She was a student in a bright white uniform, white

59

shoes and a white and blue striped tie. She had done her hair in two braids and tied them with blue ribbons ending in bows like two flowers. My eyes measured her inch by inch and came to a sudden stop when they arrived at her neck. She had a long neck that stretched in and out smoothly like a swan's, and an instant connection was made between her neck and my heart. Every time she stretched her neck and lifted up her head, my heart missed a beat.

Two minutes later, I found myself by her side. The bus arrived, and she got in and I got into the bus after her. I did not know the destination for which she had bought her ticket. So I bought a ticket to the last terminus out of the egg money I had on me. I sat four rows behind her. Her double braids, half of her neck and a part of her shoulder blade were visible to me. Half an hour later, she rang the bell and when the bus stopped, got down hurriedly and disappeared. I got off at the next stop, took another bus and came home.

No one could ever have imagined a face like that of Machal. Her skin was thick, like well-cured leather. Laughing or crying did not bring any change to it. Only her voice sounded different. When she scolded, her voice took on a false tone. She asked me, 'Where is the egg?' I said, 'It got broken.' 'But what took you so long?' 'I went back to look where it exactly broke, but I could not find the spot.'

'Where is the money?'

'That got lost as well. How many times do I have to repeat the same thing?' I breathed heavily, as if I was angry. Sometimes this trick worked. Annar was having his meal without the egg and staring at me from inside the house. We were fifteen years apart in age. If, at that moment, he'd asked me to get out of the house, I would have had to spend the night on the streets. But he did not say anything. Machal went on murmuring, 'He is only a polytechnic student, but he struts around showing off.'

It was Machal's habit to fill a china plate, which had a Chinese flower design on it, with rice and curry, cover it with another plate and leave it on the table for me. I would eat up all the rice, clearing the plate until the Chinese flowers showed up at the bottom, drink water, wash my plate, put it upside down to drain and go to bed. The sweetest sound that ever came to my ears was the sound of the plate being placed on the table. But I didn't hear the sound that day. I walked up to the table a few times and after ascertaining that there was, indeed, no plate on it, I went to bed. How difficult it must have been for a head clerk to eat a plate full of rice without an egg! I consoled myself that my discomfort was insignificant compared to my brother's tribulations, and tried to sleep. But I couldn't fall asleep for a long time.

Two days later, when Annar, content with his egg dinner, leaned his chair against the wall and sat with his legs stretched out, enjoying the cartoon in the children's section of the newspaper, I approached him and began to speak. 'I am finding this course of study difficult. There are special classes for the polytechnic course, and I would like to attend them.' Annar was taken aback. He asked me, 'How much do I have to pay?' 'No money is needed. The classes are free; I only need money for the bus fares,' I said. Annar was totally shocked that I initiated a talk about my studies and so he agreed. My brother and Machal each had wanted me to study different things. Annar wanted me to study architecture – to draw big buildings on small pieces of paper. Machal wanted me to study biology and draw small flowers on big sheets of paper. Personally, I was happy with any subject that did not require paper and pencil. I engaged all the faculties of my brain to the fullest, bought the egg for Machal in the morning and appropriated the evening hours for myself.

Anyone above the age of eighteen or nineteen will not be able to understand this account of mine. The girl came in her dazzling white uniform to that bus stop exactly at four the next afternoon. She brought a whiff of fresh air with her. Even though I kept staring at her, she never gave me a single look. Even when her eyes accidentally fell on me, her glance would pierce through me. I found that glance unbearable. Her hair confounded me – one braid would be tossed to the back, the other in front. Perhaps her idea was to adorn both her front and back equally. I felt that her beauty would not be any less even if she left both her plaits at the back. Her eyes never betrayed anger or impatience while she waited for her bus. They were always calm. They would either be lowered, looking at her shoes, or rest on the books she kept clutched to her chest. They were books on Physics, Botany and so on. From the intelligence that shone in her eyes, one could make a fair guess that she aimed to study medicine. But whenever she stretched her neck out like a swan, the act seemed to send an instant message to my heart and it skipped a beat. I always let her get into the bus first and then got in myself. She would sit in front, and I would choose a seat behind her, one that had the best view of her. At her destination, I would give her some time to walk ahead of me before I followed. She would walk on without ever turning her head. When she reached the house that had a large gate, she would open it and go in. The bottom half of the gate was covered with a tin sheet for privacy. I would walk on as if I were going to the last house on that street on an errand, then come back to take a bus home. This became a daily routine.

One day, she was not at the bus stop at 4 o'clock. I thought I would stop breathing. Six buses passed by. My heart ached, wondering if she was ill. Finally, she came at exactly 5:15. She had a badminton racket in her hand along with her books. She had wiped off all the sweat from her face and it shone even more. It was ruddier. My happiness knew no bounds. Strangely enough, the bus stop was empty that day. There was only two feet of space between us. That was a god-given opportunity for me to strike up a conversation with her. 'Do you play badminton?' I could have asked. But I did not. I could have found out what her voice was like when she opened her lips to speak. Instead, I wasted twenty minutes of that day. She once bent down and scratched her legs with her racket, in the gap between her uniform and her socks. How pretty even that little act was! I wondered if she could ever do anything that was not beautiful.

I figured that Thursdays were her badminton days. But my

mind would not let me rest even after I knew that for sure. I still went and waited at the bus stop at four as usual. On the days she carried her badminton racket, she came to the bus stop at 5:15 or 5:20. It seemed she did at times throw a glance at me, the guy who had been waiting there from 4 o'clock to look at her. But again it was the same piercing glance, as though she was looking through glass. She never seemed to notice me standing there. But I never failed even once in my duty of acting as her bodyguard; I would go back only after seeing her home safe.

One day I managed to find out which school she was in. The tie that she wore around her neck helped me. I succeeded in that endeavour by researching and collecting particulars about all the girls' schools in Colombo. Annar had, on many occasions, taunted me that my IQ never crossed the number of my shoe size. Yet, perseveringly and painstakingly, I was able to find her school. I knew where her house was located. I also knew how many people there were in her family. I came to know everything about her…the class she was in, the courses she was taking, the games she played, and so on. I knew her father's name, too; it was written on the name-plate at the gate. But I had not found out her name yet. Finally, I found that out as well.

There were advertisements in the newspapers that her school was holding a carnival. I waited eagerly for that day. She would certainly be at her school carnival. I would also get to see her in something other than the uniform she wore every day. She might wear a dress, or she might come in a sari or churidar. In my imagination, I saw her in all those clothes. When the gates to her school opened on the carnival day, I went in and searched every inch of that campus for her. Just when I was tired and about to give up after a two-hour search, I heard some voices from the counter where people competed to throw rings on to a duck's head. Two girls were in charge of that game. This girl was one of them, and with her sheer presence, she enhanced the brightness of that place.

She was in a half-sari. That was one dress I had not imagined her in. It traced perfectly the contours of her body with all its curves and lines, and prevented me from seeing anything else. The other girl worked at the table dealing with the players. My girl was doing the job of picking up the rings that fell to the ground and replacing them on the table. The shape of her body bending down to pick up the rings was etched in my mind indelibly. It was twenty-five cents for five rings. I put aside my bus fare and spent the rest buying rings and hurling them towards the duck. The ducks, very much like her, kept stretching their necks out and withdrawing them. I touched the same places on the rings that her hands had touched. I played until I had spent all the money I had. I kept looking more at her neck than at the necks of the ducks. Once, a ring that I threw went round a duck's neck, but before it could settle down the duck shook it off. The girl then laughed. Her laugh had a soft, ringing sound. She did not raise her eyes to look at me even once. The other girl called out, 'Swetha!' and that was how I learnt her name, after having spent two rupees.

Annar never opened his mouth unnecessarily. When he did, it was only to eat his boiled egg and to scold me. One day I heard him say to Machal, 'There is a great change in this boy. I never thought he would be so regular in attending the special classes.' Machal replied, 'He is up to something. You'll see.' I was amazed at how correctly she had assessed me. I couldn't decide whether I should knock my head against the wall or on the table. My mind was full of shades of red. For a year I had been escorting her home without missing a single day. I never tried to sit or stand beside her. I never smiled at her. I never gave her a love letter. It was tragic the way this love, which had grown one tiny step after another, came to an end.

If ever a day began well and proceeded without any mishap, then that surely meant something was amiss. On that particular day, even after two whole minutes had elapsed after Annar woke up, he did not resort to any harassment. Machal poured some hot soup over the hard portions of the bread that I had to eat. It even looked like there was a faint smile on her lips. She lovingly asked me to get some flour ground at the flour mill. When I came back after finishing that chore, I found a friend waiting for me at the house. Machal did not like my friends visiting me at home. I had seen the film Marma Yogi, with MGR as the hero, four times. That same MGR was visiting our city and staying at the Galle Face Hotel. My friend was there to invite me to go get a glimpse of the film star. 'He will walk out to the terrace of the hotel. We will get to see him. Let's go,' my friend said. I refused his invitation, claiming that I had some urgent business to attend to at 4 o'clock. He gave me a strange look and went away. I could see that he was suspicious as to why I would let go of a chance like this to see my favourite hero. Soon after, Machal came to the porch with her chin up in the air, as if she had a nosebleed. She spoke without parting her lips. With both her hands on her hips, she told me firmly that I could go out only after ironing her sari. Perhaps she could not do it herself because her hands were busy resting on her hips. I asked her which sari it was that she wanted ironed. She said, 'The Mysore silk one.' One could not have thought of a more severe punishment. That sari was so slippery that it kept sliding off my hands. But I managed to apply the necessary pressure once I visualized Machal between the iron and the sari. Before Machal could think of giving me another job, I made my escape to the bus stop. The bus was already moving away and I somehow ran after it and jumped in.

I sat behind her looking at her braided hair and the ribbons on it. I had never tried saying her name out loud. I didn't know how that name, starting with the mysterious sounding 'S', sounded when said out loud. But I repeated it to myself many times. As soon as she got down at the bus stop, I got down as well. For the first time, the back of her hand brushed against mine. I let her walk a little ahead and then followed her. She looked at me from the corner of her eye. I could not believe it. Never before had she done anything like that.

I do not know why, but I spent some time that day studying her closely. I committed to memory everything about her – her height, complexion, her braids, ribbons, neck, her curves, legs…everything. She walked a little faster than usual. I hurried after her as if I was trying to quickly pass by my old headmaster from school. Once she reached her house, she went in through the half-closed gates. As usual, I went to the end of the street and turned around. When I reached their gate, I was shocked to see her parents standing out there. Their faces appeared above the tin partition on the gates. I could also see her grandmother and her sister with them. The sister bent down under the partition and took a look at me. In fact, the entire family just stood there looking at me. My heart began to thud. They did not ask me anything. They did not even make a gesture towards me. But their looks! I do not know how I managed to walk past that gate, catch my bus and return home. Even in the safety of my home, my heart went on pounding intermittently against my rib cage. Annar looked at my face and asked me, 'What is it?' My reply came out in a shout: 'Nothing!' Machal must have heard it inside. It must have been heard in Wellawatte. It might have even reached MGR in his hotel.

For almost a year I travelled on the bus that she took home. If one were to calculate the distance and time I had covered, it would come to 1600 miles and 290 hours. I was very angry with that girl for the way she had treated me. But what else could she have done? I realized her predicament. If I had smiled at her, she could perhaps have turned her face away. If I had spoken to her, she might have told me that she did not like it. If I had given her a letter, she could have torn it into pieces in front of me and expressed her displeasure.

But I followed her silently, and she too showed defiance in the same manner. She must have been a good girl.

'Papa, that ant has crossed Nigeria,' my son said.

'Okay, but leave it alone.'

Stretching across the entire surface of the table, drawn on the glass top, was a map of the world. Since it was a map drawn during the reign of the British, some countries that had just come into existence were not on it. The ant was crawling on the map. My son's finger followed it.

'The ant has now reached Italy.'

'Right.'

'Papa, have you ever travelled?'

'Sort of.'

'Where did you go?'

'To some place.'

'How far was it, Papa?'

'1600 miles.'

'When did you go?'

'When I was seventeen years old.'

'How long did it take for you to get there?'

'290 hours; that would make twelve days.'

'Twelve days!'

'Twelve days, my son, is not all that long a time to discover truth.'

Without taking part in our conversation, all by itself, the ant was crossing the Atlantic Ocean.

eight

Use Your Brains!

WHEN THEY WERE IN school, they would cling to each other. I'd known for a long time that Samantha and Alec were lovers. I was one of the girls who looked forward to the day they'd break up, because Alec was so very handsome. He was Ukrainian, tall and blue-eyed; his curls falling on his brow, and his satchel hanging from one of his shoulders. He would come into the school swaying, dreamy-eyed, as if he had woken up only seconds ago.

Our class had students from various countries. Many of us had come to Canada as refugees. Samantha, however, was Canadian. She had the right to love anybody. Alec had come here as a refugee as well. The least she could have done was to leave him for one of us. But it did not seem as if their love affair would end any time soon. This was the third affair for Samantha, and no one knew how many love affairs Alec might already have had. He had been here for just one year.

Canada's daylight saving time always confused and exasperated me. On that day, dawn appeared to overlap with the night. The day appeared before the night was done. And Mama had begun her tireless nagging even before I had shaken off my sleep fully. She had plenty of words of advice, all leftovers from the day before. 'Use your brains,' she always cautioned. If a girl needed to get things done, she had two choices: one was to use her brains, and the other was, well, to use another part of the female anatomy. She never mentioned what that part was. 'Don't you come late like you did yesterday! You better be home before I get here, and clean the house and wash the plates. I will cook our meal as soon as I get back from work. You may then do your schoolwork,' she instructed me.

There were times when I felt sad for Mama. I was born within a year of Mama's moving to Canada. When I was five years old, Mama got a divorce. As her settlement, she got the two-bedroom house that Papa had bought with his savings. The very mention of Papa would send her into a rage. He had left her for another woman.

But I have fond memories of Papa. When I was a child, he would throw me up in the air and catch me. If he was lying on the bed, I would climb on to his chest and play there. Once, a swing in the park hit me on my forehead and I shed a few drops of blood. I remember vividly how Papa panicked, picked me up and ran home. The other memory I have of him was at the dining table. One day at dinner, a fight broke out between Papa and Mama. He pulled Mama by the hair and shouted. I got scared and began to bawl. The next-door neighbour called the police and they took Papa away. He never came home after that. Mama removed all his photos that had been hanging on the walls. But I have a snapshot of him stuck in the inside flap of my diary. Mama does not know about it. Though it is now ten years since he left us, that photo keeps the memory of him alive.

After many days, Alec spoke to me for the first time ever. The heads of other girls turned towards me in envy. He called me 'Ann'. My name is Anushuya, can you believe it? I do not know from where Mama dug up this name. But my classmates called me Ann.

I looked at Samantha. Her eyes were ablaze with anger.

'Oh! Isn't your name Alec? And are you not in the same class as me?' I said sarcastically.

'I can see you are making fun of me,' he said. 'Ann, you are the cleverest in our class. Can you help me learn about isotopes?'

'That depends on what I get in return,' I replied. The conversation would have continued had the bell not rung.

The following morning Mama looked rather worried. Fearing it might set her off on one of her endless tirades, I did not probe for a reason. But she eventually told me in her own way. 'Our manager has left the firm, and a new one has come in his place. From the day he took charge of the office, he has been threatening to dismiss me. His harassment is endless. I do not feel like going to work. But if I don't work we will be on the streets.' Something prompted me to lend

Mama the high-heeled shoes that I usually wore only to parties. Standing in them, Mama looked tall and pretty. She said she would wear them to work that day. Suddenly she gave me a big hug and a kiss. And that's when I realized that she was kissing me after many years. I just ran to school without turning back to look at her.

I do not know how to rate the day; was it good or bad? When my friends saw me coming into the class, they stopped talking. That upset me and made me sad. Like a soldier turning his head in a parade, Alec walked in single file with other students, but his eyes were glued to me all the time. His gaze continued to be on me until the classes were over. That made me very happy.

Nobody will believe what happened at school the following day. Alec came to school wearing dark glasses. They reflected twin images of me. When he walked towards me, it looked as if I was approaching myself. I asked him to remove his glasses, but he refused. He said, 'In ancient days, the Chinese soldier had a mirror hanging on his chest. Any enemy soldier on the battlefield would be forced to look into it, and stop fighting.'

'Do you think I am going to kill you?' I asked him.

'Aren't you doing that every day?' he replied.

We were in the playground and were absolutely stunned at the sight awaiting us there during the break. Hundreds of Canada geese had gathered there, filling the area with their loud cackles. They were migrating south during the month of October. They had stopped midway for a breather.

They were so intent on feeding on the grass and chasing insects that even when you walked through the flock, they mechanically made way for you without flying away. I stood in their midst, and Alec photographed me with the geese. He told me that he had a silver dollar coin inscribed with a flying Canada goose issued in commemoration of Canada's centenary celebrations but I did not believe him. He said he'd bring the coin and show it to me some day.

Something strange happened that afternoon. While waiting at the bus stop, I was shocked at what I saw across the road. It was my father, after all these years. In a tattered coat, he was walking with his head bent down, as if he was looking for some coins on the ground. My heart froze at his beggarly appearance. I remembered Mama saying once that he had lost his job. Here we were living comfortably in the house that Papa had built with his hard work. I thought of crossing to the other side of the road and giving him the ten dollar bill I had on me. I could, perhaps, give him an unexpected hug and kiss as well. How happy his face would have looked then! But I was not sure if I should do that. My bus came just then, and I climbed in. I kept looking at Papa's photo for quite some time after I got home. I did not say anything about the incident to Mama.

The next day we had a lot of fun in class. We were all asked to sing the national anthems of our native countries. I was born in Canada, but there were many in my class who were born in different countries. The Canadians sang their national anthem in a chorus. The Japanese students sang theirs, but even before we could straighten ourselves and get ready to give our full attention to the song, it was over. It must be the shortest anthem in the world! Fortunately, there was no Uruguay national in our class. Their national song was supposed to be the longest, but it was also sweet on the ears, I was told. Alec sang the Ukrainian anthem in all its musical glory. Looking at him then, I could not help but think that he would have looked handsome even if he had not sung but just moved his lips. Savithri and I had planned to sing the Sri Lankan national song, but instead, sang the first two lines of a famous Tamil movie song, 'Manmatha Rasa, Manmatha Rasa'. It did sound very much like the anthem of a country that produced large numbers of refugees. Nobody ever found out. We were rewarded with terrific applause.

Next morning Mama caught me red-handed. I cannot for the life of me guess how she found out about my using make-up, styling my hair and then hiding the lipstick among my books. She had somehow got wind of it all. 'It is not good that you spend so much time putting on your make-up. Are you going to that school to study or for something else? Use your brains. Don't you ever forget that,' she said. Mama constantly surprised me with such sudden outbursts.

At school, I saw Samantha walking fast. I nudged Savithri, who was standing next to me, and told her, 'Just you wait, Samantha will drop her books to the ground now.' And so she did. As she bent down to pick up her books from the ground, her striped skirt rode up at the back. Her rounded bottom, which could be the envy of any girl, was turned purposefully in Alec's direction. As she groped to pick up her books, her eyes strayed, looking for Alec. Then she gave me a look. It was a real wonder that her eyes could display both love and hate at the same time.

I do not think I can ever forget what happened later that day; I will remember it even after twenty years. When I wanted to go home halfway through my classes, Alec wanted to come with me. He wanted to have a one-on-one lesson on isotopes. As I put my key into the lock and opened the door of my house, he asked me, 'What's that smell?' I was ashamed to say anything in reply, for it was the lingering smell of the curry Mama had cooked some three days back. I took him straight to the basement and switched on the tubelight. It came on after a minute. He flung his backpack, stretched himself on the sofa and asked for a drink. He had been there for barely a minute, and already it was as if he owned the place. I walked upstairs with a silent prayer in my heart that I should find some drink in there, and opened the fridge. I was lucky. Behind a half-eaten apple there was a can of Coke. I brought it down and, like a submissive wife, handed it to him. He opened the can and began to sip from it leisurely, as if it was expensive wine. I took that opportunity to hurriedly remove the photographs that were there of my mother in a sari and with the red dot on her forehead.

'Take out your book,' I said. His eyes were riveted on my body. I was wondering if the part of my anatomy his eyes were seeking was the one that Mama referred to constantly in her innuendoes. I felt like I was standing in a doctor's room, wearing a paper dress, and a sort of shyness crept over me. I tried to hide it, and opening my book to page twenty-four, began, 'Isotope is a mineral with similar qualities but different weights...' But suddenly he put his face on my shoulder and began to sniff. I held on to my book with one hand and pushed him away with the other. He brought out his cell phone and showed me the snap he had taken of me in my black and white uniform, standing amidst the black and white Canada geese. 'You, too, look like a fattened goose,' he said and laughed. As he turned his phone sideways, my image turned as well. I did look beautiful.

There was ample space on the sofa but he sat very close to me. He put his hand in his pocket and said, 'See, I remembered. I have brought this to show you.' He took the goose-inscribed silver coin out of his pocket. It was a rare and valuable one. I turned it over in my hand and looked at the other side. It had Queen Elizabeth on it. 'Is this yours?' I asked. 'I love to collect coins,' he said.

'What else do you like?'

'Your stone-studded eardrops.' His lips came close to my ears. He caught my eardrop with his mouth as if he were going to eat it up. 'Hey! What are you doing? What are you up to?' He began to squeeze my shoulder blades in the opposite direction, as if trying to open them. Just then, as if on cue, I could hear someone insert the key into the keyhole and open the front door. It was still some three hours before Mama was expected home. A burglar, perhaps? I could hear my heart beat; I slowly climbed up two steps and peeped into the lounge. It was Mama. A male form, too, came up the steps stealthily and went upstairs.

'Who's that?' asked Alec in a conspiratorial voice. 'You fool! That's my mother. You leave now. Get out through the basement window,' I pleaded.

He first threw his backpack out of the window. The sound of Mama's laughter came from upstairs. 'Why is your mother laughing?' he asked. 'You go now. She's like that. She rarely laughs these days. Just so she does not completely forget how to laugh, she practises when she is alone.' After he had put his head and feet out of the window and jumped out, he shouted, 'My Coke!' I handed him the can he had been drinking from. Slinging his bag over his shoulder, he left, sipping his Coke and waving to me. 'Bopasya!' he said as he turned to me one last time. In Ukrainian, 'bopasya' means goodbye. Something told me that he wouldn't ever come back.

He would never know that my computer password was his name. It felt like the world was coming to an end. I could hear two pairs of footsteps above me. Mama laughed again. This was a different kind of laugh. All of a sudden, a strange thought came into my head. Mama and I were isotopes of the same element; substances with the same qualities but of different weights!

I lay down on the sofa in the exact same place where Alec had stretched himself just a few minutes ago, and stared at the roof. The time had come for me to use my brains.

nine

The Horoscope

PAPA HAD GREAT expectations from life. So, as soon as his children were born, he had their horoscopes made by the famous astrologer of our village. We were seven siblings. Horoscopes for each of us were written in separate notebooks. Papa had all of them bundled up and locked in a wooden chest. We could neither peer at, nor pore over them.

We were all born in our house. As if by prior agreement, we were all born at night time. A midwife took care of all of Mama's deliveries. Some time during the evening, Mama would begin to speak of the piercing pains in her middle. Papa would spring into action immediately. He had three duties. Only one house in our village boasted of a timepiece; it could be set in motion by winding it. Papa would borrow the clock so that the exact time of birth of his children could be properly recorded.

The second task involved a steel folding spring cot that lay in the cattle shed. Papa would bring the cot into the house, set it up, spread a cotton mattress on it, and make Mama lie down on it. The mattress, when spread out on the lax springs that ran across the cot, would sag in the middle. Mama could lower herself down into that hollow on her own, but if she needed to get out of it, it took two persons to haul her out. That cot was a heritage piece from Papa's family. He was born on that cot. So he believed the cot brought them luck. That we survived childbirth was not because we were smart, or because Mama was strong. It could not even be attributed to the midwife's skill. It was all only because of that lucky cot. Or so my father believed.

Papa's third task, of course, was to send word to the midwife. No birth went astray while that midwife was in charge. For every male child she delivered, she would be paid fifty cents, and if it was a girl she got less than that. The delivery would take place in a room that was screened off with a bamboo mat. Since the lamp that lit the room used neem oil, a particular kind of smell pervaded the room. The midwife would take charge of the room, and Papa would stay outside. Around midnight or some time after that, when the baby arrived, his or her cries would be heard outside. Papa would then look at the clock and write the exact time in a notebook, wetting the pencil tip with his tongue. The astrologer would go by that time when drawing the horoscope.

It was through family gossip that I came to know of all these procedures. I was very tiny then. I did not even know how to bite into a banana; I could only nibble at the side.

When my sister was born, I got to witness the whole thing. She was the seventh child, the last. This was a matter of wonder to the people of our village. The normal count in any family was ten or twelve children. Many assumed that after a succession of boys, when the girl finally arrived, the couple must have decided they had had enough. But neither Papa nor Mama was motivated by any such consideration. It was revealed later that an astrologer was responsible for their decision.

In those days, it was the custom to roll out a lemon from the delivery room when the baby was born. The midwife in charge always had a lemon at hand. As soon as the baby arrived, she would roll it out of the room. The time the fruit came out was usually registered and used to cast the horoscope. But Papa did not have much faith in this fruit-rolling method. He would wait for the first cries of the baby. He contended that the wail was enough to give him the time of birth. Mama's vote was for the fruit. However, the accident that followed my birth made Papa change his stand.

Mama had complained of some activity inside her stomach around four in the afternoon and had gone to lie down on the cot inside the room. Papa waited outside with his notebook, pencil and tongue. Our dog, Veeman, lay by Papa's side, his chin on the floor and his eyes turned upwards. The midwife stood by Mama's side as she screamed deliriously in pain. But I would not come out. The midwife had tried all the tricks that she knew. Dawn was soon to break and light would push away the darkness of night. All of a sudden a little pink foot

81

peeped out. It would take a few more seconds for the other foot to emerge. Birds raised a hue and cry with demands for the day to break. The midwife took the risk of dragging me out by my foot and I got born. Usually when babies are born, they arrive on their chest in a swimming position. I was on my back, looking up at the sky. I had the desire to be different and innovative even then! My face was covered with a membrane. I had decided not to breathe, so the midwife had to turn me upside down and give me a good shake and pat my back. But nothing seemed to work. Only when a hot needle pricked me on my forehead and chest did I let out my first cries. Papa, unaware of these goings-on inside the room, heard me cry, and promptly noted down that time as the time of my birth.

Until I was about twelve years old, I proudly showed off the streaks on my forehead and chest to my classmates in school. Then gradually the marks faded away. The astrologer drew up my horoscope with the time Papa had provided. He said that since I had come out with my face turned up, looking skywards, my birth was unique and I would attain fame. For a while the people in my house believed this and held me in high esteem. But very soon it was discovered that my horoscope was faulty. Since the midwife had been foolish enough to waste her time in reviving me instead of paying attention to the correct time of my arrival, my horoscope ended up being inaccurate. And from then on, I led a colourless life, absolutely clueless as to what I would become when I grew up.

Later, when my younger brother and sister were born, the fruit-rolling method was revived. The midwife was handed a lemon and instructed to roll it out. There were risks inherent in this method. The midwife might forget to do her duty, or she might roll it a wee bit too fast and it might roll off out of our sight. But thankfully, no such accidents happened, and their horoscopes were duly registered, right and proper. Papa piled all of them one on top of another and locked them securely in the chest.

The horoscope that was talked about in glowing terms every now and then was Annan's. The astrologer had predicted that Annan, my eldest brother, would become a great judge. This gave my parents immense joy. I heard them speak highly of Annan's horoscope to neighbours and relatives. As far as they were concerned, Annan was already on his way to becoming a judge. Annan, meanwhile, repeated the eighth grade a second time.

There were many who thought that my Mama's and Papa's horoscopes were a perfect match. But I was the only one who knew the truth. One night I had spread a mat in the veranda outside, intending to sleep there. Mama rarely let me sleep there, but somehow, I had convinced her. Other times when I had slept there, in the morning I would find a bloodied leech sticking to my skin. It would be difficult to identify whose blood it was, the leech's or mine. Anyway, that particular night, I lay there as if asleep, listening to Papa talking to a visiting relative who had come from somewhere far off. It was then that I came to know that the credit for getting Papa

83

married to Mama went to a lizard. Papa, whose first wife had died, had been in a dilemma as to whether to take Mama as his second wife or not. Climbing on to a wall of a temple, he had vowed that he would come down from his perch only if the gods gave him their permission. As morning moved to noon and noon to evening, he waited. And then he heard a lizard's click. Papa took that as the divine signal, jumped off the wall and agreed to marry Mama. If that lizard had not made that cry of hunger, Mama would not have married Papa, we would not have been born, and Papa would not have had the good fortune to bundle up a pile of horoscopes and keep them safe locked in a chest.

I once asked Papa how horoscopes were cast before the invention of clocks. We had to bide our time to approach him with such questions. There were occasions when he would begin to sing, keeping time by slapping on his thigh. Those were the times to ask our questions for he was in a happy mood. He told us that if babies were born during the day, the exact time could be calculated by measuring one's shadow with one's feet. I have myself witnessed this. As for the night, there were people in the village who could tell the time by looking at the position of the stars. Astrologers would go by the time that these people had noted down.

There was also another method to tell the time for horoscopes. Day or night, as soon as the baby arrived, they would cut a banana stem right across. Every house had banana trees in those days. The day after, or even two days later, the astrologer would come and measure the growth of the plant in the intervening time, and thus calculate the time of birth and cast the horoscope.

In our house, the timepiece would disappear the day after Mama's delivery. Papa would fold and put the steel cot back in the cowshed. Mama would be up, returning to her chores gradually. A new hammock would be found hanging from the roof. It was not uncommon to see two hammocks at the same time if the children had come in rapid succession with just a year's or a year-and-a-half's gap between them. The strong smell of burning neem oil would envelop the entire house. The thirty-first day would be the day of purification. Preparations for the next baby would begin in earnest.

Any astrologer who passed through our village never left without paying our house a visit. Papa would bring out the horoscope bundle from the box and hand it over to him. He would analyse the horoscopes and come up with predictions that would satisfy all those waiting to know their fate. When all the horoscopes had been analysed, Mama would turn her eyes towards Papa. Papa would then speak.

'Please look at the eldest boy's horoscope carefully. Will he become a judge?'

The astrologer would go back to the horoscope and begin noting down some figures and calculations on the back of the notebook. 'Ha! This aspect escaped my notice! I have never seen another horoscope which had Mercury in such an exalted position. Mercury is the lord of education. Your son is sure to become a judge,' he would say. That day the astrologer would be treated to a special feast.

Many such astrologers came to our house. They were all cheats, and none of them contradicted what the earlier ones had said. I think there was some sort of understanding among them. Once, what I saw when I woke up at midnight gave me the shivers. A young astrologer with a large kumkum dot on his forehead and matted hair all spread out was sitting in front of a lamp, poring over the horoscopes. The front half of Papa's head that was bald shone like an upturned cockroach. Mama was chewing the betel nut with her front teeth. Her head was drooping like a withered flower. Her fingers had curled up on her cheek. Though they were sitting very near me, they seemed to be somewhere far off, immersed in their thoughts.

'The demons get their strength at night. So children born at night possess some demonic qualities. Even Lord Krishna of the Mahabharata was endowed with such qualities and that was what helped him slay Kamsa, the demon king. Not that it is a serious drawback. But seven children have been born in your house, one after another, during those dark hours. The demonic aspect is thick in this house.' In a soft voice, half-poetry and half-prose, he pronounced these words, and lifted his arm up, spreading it out as if he was setting a bird free.

Papa and Mama were thunderstruck by this oracle. Papa asked in a quivering voice, 'Is there anything we can do to nullify this effect?'

'Some rituals can be done later on. But another baby should not be born at night here. The house will not be able to bear that,' he said in an authoritative voice.

'So what is to be done now?'

He replied, 'It would be better if you could have a couple of your children staying away from this house and continue their studies elsewhere.'

That was how my second brother went to stay at Aunt's house. There was talk of enrolling me in a boarding school and then suddenly it was done. The day before I was scheduled to leave home, I went into the kitchen and saw my mother sitting in front of the lamp all by herself and crying. When I asked her why she was crying, she silently wiped her face with the end of her sari. But tears continued to flow even as she kept wiping them away. No sound came out of her. That was the last time we were all together as a family in that house.

The demons that the astrologer had predicted did not emerge from within the house. They came from outside. Their feet were inside thick leather boots that marched to the rhythm of gunshots. Houses, streets, playgrounds went silent. The earth and sky were transformed. Veeman, our dog, ran away from home and never came back. My parents did not live long enough to see Annan become anything. Twice, Annan was caught by the police and had to go to the court for breaking the law. The prediction that he would rise in life as a judge went wrong, and he climbed the steps of the court only as an accused.

I write this at night from Toronto. 'Nights are not for humans. They are the hours that belong to the demons. They cause us harm' – Papa and Mama had told me this many times. But how do I determine when night begins and when it ends? Right now, it is midnight for me here. It is the beginning of the night in California. In England, it is early morning and in Ceylon, it is already tomorrow.

The bundle of horoscopes that Papa had once so carefully guarded comes to my mind. Our horoscopes were cast on the basis of the time that the borrowed timepiece showed. But we, the true owners of those horoscopes, could never lay our hands on them. It now occurs to me that I should have tried to take a look at them at least once. All of us children were born at night from the womb of the same mother, delivered by the same midwife, on the same iron cot. When we scrambled off in different directions, we lost touch with everything. We have no clue whatsoever about what happened to the horoscopes that Papa treasured. Today we live in different countries, under varied circumstances, harbouring our individual sorrows. Some gathered speed and crossed the boundaries. Some stopped right on reaching the target. Some did not even reach the door.

ten

After Yesterday

CANADA BAFFLED MAMA in many ways. What struck her most was that bolts and locks did not have any real function in the houses in Canada. In her Colombo house, bolts and locks were everywhere – on the gate, door and every other lockable object. Mama's cupboard had a lock, her wooden chest could be locked, even the table drawers had their own locks and, of course, all storage boxes could be, and were, locked. The front door and the main entrance were certainly secured with a big, tortoise-shaped lock. The place, in short, had innumerable locks, and the residents were all safe.

In Mama's view, it was an unpardonable lapse that even the refrigerators in Canada had no locks. Mama had been under the impression that all fridges came with locks. It perhaps came from that one memorable visit of hers to a friend's house in Colombo. The fridge of that house was displayed in the lounge and seemed to actively participate in their conversation. It came alive at times and made some noises. And then it went silent when it felt like it. But what Mama liked most about that fridge was the lock. The way the hostess unlocked her fridge and took out various things was quite an impressive and expansive gesture. But in Canada, the contraption had no lock. Moreover, the thing itself was kept out of the public eye! How on earth would visitors to the house know that there was a fridge if it was hidden inside the kitchen!

The next problem was the bathroom. Why it could not be locked was simply beyond Mama's comprehension. But she would have forgiven that fact had the door at least shut properly. When you closed the door behind you, it somehow came alive on its own, and when you stepped out of the shower, there it was, gaping at you, its mouth wide open. In Mama's view, that door definitely needed a lock, or one had to give up bathing. One day, without a word to me, Mama went to my bookshelf and picked up all three volumes of Chellpapa's *Thirst for Freedom*. My respect for my mother increased threefold, but I wondered how she could read all three volumes simultaneously and in a short time. But her intentions turned out to be quite different. When she came out of her bath, her face displayed a deep sense of relief.

'Did you like the books?' I asked her.

'They are not thick enough to keep the door properly shut. We need thicker books,' she said.

Until Mama brought it to my attention, I had quite

forgotten that the main door of the house needed to be locked, which meant that it had to have bolts. Of course, in our street in Colombo, all houses had bolts, one on the inside of the door and one on the outside. When we retired for the night, we would lock the bolts from inside. And when we went out of the house, we would secure the outside bolt with a lock. I always dreaded our family outings. Mama would secure the bolt with the 'tortoise' lock, which was as big as a coconut. She would then give the lock quite a few tugs before she would finally consider leaving. We would follow her. We would not have gone about a hundred yards, when something would bother Papa and he would retrace his steps, and would hold and hang from the tortoise lock with all his strength to ensure that it was, indeed, firmly bolted and locked. Only then would we resume our journey.

Mama insisted that we should fit our front door in my house in Canada with a bolt like the one at home. She complained that she was not able to sleep properly at nights and that bad dreams haunted her. I told her, 'Nobody has bolts on doors in Canada. The houses have burglar alarms. If any thief is bold enough to enter the house, the alarm will go off.'

'How does that work? Will the alarm begin its wails before the thief enters the house or after he is in?'

'It starts ringing only after the thief is inside the premises,' I told her.

'What use would that be? Should it not alert you before the thief enters the house?' she asked.

I did not have any answer for that. So I took Mama bolt-shopping one day. Some of the shopkeepers did not even know what bolts were. Even those who were familiar with the word had not heard of bolts that were used to lock up houses. Finally in an antique shop we managed to find two huge bolts that belonged to the previous century. Mama fell in love with them. Only after they were fixed to the door could Mama sleep peacefully.

But I lost my peace. Whenever the telephone rang, Mama could not stay quiet; she had to rush to pick up the receiver. Look, in Canada no one picked up the calls that came through the landline; it was merely ornamental. It would ring often and cheer up the house. That was all that was expected of it. But I could not get Mama to understand this.

Our house was narrow, but what it lacked in width it made up in length. It stretched out so long that often the weather at the entrance would not be the same as that at the rear. But all that distance did not matter to Mama. She never gave up. As soon as she heard the telephone ring, she would come running as if she were in a race, and pick up the receiver. But in all her huffing and puffing and panting, she wouldn't even be able to say 'Hello' in one breath. She would begin, 'He...' into the mouthpiece, panting, then take a deep breath and conclude with, 'Lo'!

My friends called me on my cell phone, as I never used the landline. I kept it only for the calls from the marketing people, the wrong numbers and for those who constantly requested donations. Not only did they persist in their calling, they also persevered in leaving voice messages for me. Every Sunday at about ten in the morning, I would listen to all the messages on the landline and erase them one by one. That would take me about half an hour. But Mama would have none of this. She continued to run to answer the calls. In fact, she thought it was her duty to do that.

I asked her once, 'Mama, why do you run so hurriedly as if your life depended on it?'

She replied, 'Son, it could be you calling me, no? I thought it might be you ringing to ask me if I had made venthayak curry for lunch.' I had no answer for that.

While I persisted in asking her not to bother with the ringing of the telephone, I failed to teach her how to handle the ringing of the doorbell. One day, back from an outing, I paused at the entrance to the house when I heard loud noises and laughter coming from inside. I even checked the number of the house, wondering if I had come to the wrong address. When I entered, I found three visitors sitting with Mama. There was a man in a grey coat, which was all crumpled, its collar frayed at the edges; he must have been around fifty. There was a short woman, also in a grey dress, with a scarf tied around her head. The third one was a younger woman who had taken up half the sofa. Both women wore grey, unattractive clothes, which were shapeless, with no pleats or frills. The fabric they were made out of bore a strong resemblance to sack cloth. I recognized them instantly as preachers who went from door to door looking for supporters.

When the girl introduced herself to me, all I could

focus on was her strange footwear, which was shaped like a crocodile's head. Even without my asking her, she told me that she was fourteen years old. She was the largest fourteen-year-old I had seen until then. Placing her arms on her thighs, she lowered her eyes for a moment and raised them up theatrically. With one finger, she twirled a lock of hair on her shoulder. Notwithstanding her gunny sack clothes, at that moment she seemed strangely attractive. I felt the blood rush in my veins. The man cleared his throat every now and then, a sound very similar to the one that a dog makes when lapping up water. He had all the qualifications that a preacher needed. He picked up his conversation with Mama from where he had left off. Mama listened attentively to those uninvited guests with great love. On the table were scattered books, magazines and flyers. She looked at the man without ever taking her eyes off him. It was the way a calf would look at its mother.

Such people were never to be entertained in the house. But if they ever trespassed, then there were certain rules to follow while you put up with them. I was trying to see how to regain control of the situation, but it appeared that their interaction had acquired a pattern even before I arrived. In his squeaky voice, the preacher would deliver a long sentence. Then he would test Mama by asking her to repeat what he had said. Like a third grade student obeying her teacher, Mama would repeat whatever he had said. In fact, she even imitated his rendition of the sentence by raising her voice a little at the end of her delivery. I thought the preacher had found a new disciple. That young girl kept swinging her feet up and down. I was waiting to see her raise and lower her eyes again. That was the only reason I kept my irritation in check.

After they had left, I pounced on Mama and asked her, 'How could you just invite them into the house?' Her face fell.

'What are you saying?' she asked. 'They are not ordinary people. They are all white people.'

It was Mama's unshakeable belief that white people never stole, never told lies and never killed people.

Eventually, my anger completely died down. A few weeks later, I was at the dining table, and Mama, as usual, was standing by the table. Food that could be cooked in half an hour took half a day in Mama's hands. She would never sit at the table with me. She insisted on serving the food like a waitress in a restaurant. The dish could be just inches away from me, but she had to serve the food on to my plate. She wouldn't eat with me. Her job was to keenly observe the way my face contorted in the relishing of her food.

Mama began gently. 'Son, do you know the name of the god of those who have attained salvation?'

'No, I don't,' I replied.

'The world's first god was Yahweh. That's a Hebrew word. That language has no vowels. All the letters are consonants. So you are allowed to pronounce it any way you want. But god's true name appeared even before Hebrew was discovered. That name is Tetragrammaton. Those who take that name of the primordial god go to heaven when they die. They have promised me that they will pray for me.'

That was the year they declared that Pluto was not a planet. That was the year when the Sri Lanka peace talks in Geneva broke down. That was the year winter arrived early in Toronto without any warning, and the trees quickly shed their leaves. Instead of thick winter clothing, Mama was in thin overalls stained with splashes of curry. She did not seem to mind the slight shivers her body went into. She put both her arms across her shoulders and looking at my knees, said, 'I want to go home.' I did not show any opposition. Her reasons could have been Tetragrammaton, or the food, or the fact that she could not properly put her skirt out to dry in the open air.

Mama's love for cooking was boundless. She wanted to get up early in the morning and light the stove like she used to do back in her country. She refused to believe that Canadians never spent more than half an hour of a day in the kitchen. She never once lifted the serving ladle without making an instant conversion of the prices of groceries from Canadian dollars to Sri Lankan rupees and wondering at the enormous difference between the two. Whenever she referred to the dishes she had cooked for the day, she would always include their prices. 'I fried 8000 rupees worth of fish today,' or, 'I have cooked tomatoes worth 800 rupees today.' That would be the way she would tell me the day's menu.

It has been a month since Mama went back home. She came ten thousand miles to Canada with great enthusiasm, but she returned to Colombo confused and with her fervour diminished. I sometimes wonder whether I was too harsh with her during her stay. Once Mama had hung her skirt out to dry at the back of the house and my neighbour filed a complaint and made quite an issue of it. 'I have dried my skirt on the clothesline in the garden of my house. Did I drop it on his head?' Mama grumbled for a whole day. She could not understand what the problem was. Her eyes were wet and shining. She must have decided that very day that she wanted to return home. That was, perhaps, the last straw.

Mama had been greatly troubled by my requests that she not answer the telephone when it rang, that the fridge was not to be locked, doors were not be interfered with, skirts could not be dried, unknown guests were not to be invited and entertained...Perhaps all these rules were something Mama could not cope with.

I still remember the question she asked me at the airport just before she left.

'Do you erase all the messages on your telephone every Sunday morning at ten?'

I said, 'Yes, I do.'

'Don't forget to listen to the messages before you erase them,' she said.

I did not understand why she said that. While she kissed me, she patted my back and said, 'May Yahweh bless you.' I touched her cheek. Even as I was wondering how my palm got wet, she disappeared through the security gate with her yellow handbag. For a second I could see the edge of her thin shoulder. Then that too went out of sight.

Around seven in the evening, there was a knock on my door. I wondered who could be knocking on the door instead of ringing the bell. I never have any visitors at that hour. I opened the door hurriedly and saw three figures standing close to the door. They were no strangers; they were the all too familiar preachers. The gentleman with his wife and the daughter who claimed she was fourteen years old.

The three were dressed in the same colour and manner as before. He had a ladies' handbag in his hand. He spoke close to my mouth, 'Is your mother in?' His teeth, halfway through the handiwork of a dentist, looked huge. I folded my leg and planted it crosswise at the door and said, 'Mama has gone back to Colombo.'

'I see!' he said, then to surprise me even more, crossed my leg as in an obstacle race and entered the house. He sat down on the chair where I had been sitting, reading my *Toronto Star*, and nodded at me, indicating I take a seat as well. His wife calmly spread out the literature they had brought with them on the table. The girl who had claimed she was a fourteen-year-old sat on the sofa, giving it a nice pressing down. It sank down by a foot. She sat there with her knees together, her shoulders thrust backwards and her crocodile footwear pointed forward.

The preacher said, 'Your mother is a noble lady.' The other two nodded their heads in agreement.

'She was familiar with Yahweh,' he said.

'Is that so?'

'Would you like to go to heaven?' he asked, looking at me as if he had a ticket to spare for me.

'Sure!'

'Do you know how to go there?'

'If you tell me at what intersection it is, I will somehow find my way,' I said.

His face now was not what it was when he knocked at the door and entered the house. His eyes shone red, like those of a nocturnal animal. His wife stuffed the books, journals and leaflets into her bag in a hurry. As if someone had issued her a command, the supposedly fourteen-year-old girl sprang up, and before the seat could regain its original shape, she covered the distance to the entrance and stood at the door.

Still seated, the man's body kept sinking lower and lower, reminding me of the way a dog crouches when it is angry. His breath was loud enough for me to hear it. I think he was taking great pains not to lose control of himself. 'Your mother is a very honourable and noble lady. We shall continue to pray to make sure that she goes to heaven.'

I asked, 'Is there any fee to be paid?' He stood up suddenly. The muscles on his face stood out and could be seen individually. Without opening his lips and without looking at my face, he said goodbye through clenched teeth and dashed outside. He opened the door of my house and shut it with a loud bang in my face, as if he was closing the gates of heaven on me. The three disappeared.

After Mama left, for the first time I locked the door and secured the bolt before I went to bed.

eleven

Borrow One!

I WAS OF THE AGE when I believed that a car would go all on its own if I kept touching the steering wheel. I was probably eight or nine and I would do anything in the world just for an ice-cream. When they give you a round glass cup filled to the brim with ice-cream and top it with a soft red cherry, it looks lavishly beautiful and tastes much more delicious. In a way lying is also like that. Every lie needs to be spiked with a tiny bit of truth. Great lies are manufactured like that. I knew this when I was four years old. The thrill, fun and playfulness I experienced when uttering a lie I never got from anything else.

The rules at my parents' house were very confusing. Whatever tasted lousy was deemed good for my health. Castor oil was good, bitter gourd very good and spinach was supposedly the best. Heaven forbid we should put any of these in our mouths! Ice-cream – now that is really yummy, chocolate is delicious. Sugared twisties, once you start you can never stop eating them. Unfortunately these goodies were banned. Even when my mother made sugared twisties at home, those were locked up and kept out of reach on one of the top shelves. Despite this precaution, these delicacies kept steadily decreasing. Witnessing the speed at which I pilfered them, my brother would say, 'Easy bro, at this rate the twisties will go straight into your head.' I didn't worry too much about getting caught. I had a bunch of lies at hand.

There is a method to crafting lies. I told a whole lot of them to my class teacher at school. This wasn't intentional. He would ask something, and lies would just flow out as soon as I opened my mouth. But in the instances where I didn't get caught, all the thrill, fun and excitement engendered by the lie gave me all the reason I needed to continue.

'Why haven't you done your homework?' the teacher would ask.

'Our goat ate it, sir!'

The poor soul would fall for it. At home, Mom would ask: 'Why so late? Your brother arrived a long time back.'

'During the 12 o'clock puja the Padmanabha priest fainted.' Only the 12 o'clock part was true.

Several important incidents in my life occurred when I was nine years old. One morning Mom was suffering from a severe stomach ache. My father beckoned me in a thundering voice. At times, when he screamed we could almost hear the echo as well. 'Run fast to the midwife's house and fetch her now,' he ordered. School-dress, house-dress, outside-dress and night-dress were all one and the same for me, so I left as I was, in a hurry. I was a sloth only at home, but outside I was a sprinter. All along the way, the streets were lined with tamarind trees that were laden with fruit. I plucked a few low-hanging ones and ate them. At the edges of the fence stood termite hills; some of them were even taller than me. The day before yesterday, I had seen a snake come out of those very hills. As I hurried past that dreadful spot I was brought to a sudden halt. Sniffing the ground, a stray dog stood ominously. It owned the street and had chased me several times before. It looked at me through narrowed eyes and snarled. It would surely chase me if I took off. Luckily a tall old man came walking by, holding a hen upside down by its feet. I grabbed his other hand and started walking alongside him. Forgetting its hostility, the dog started to lick itself and lay down.

The old man had to bend down to peer at me and I had to stretch my neck backwards to get a glimpse of him, as if I were looking at a plane. Only after his lips had stopped moving did his words reach my ears.

'How old are you?' he asked.

Usually folks asked me my name first. 'I am twelve,' I replied.

I think he believed it. 'How about you, how old are you?' I asked.

'I have three dhotis, one shirt, two shawls, one decorative upper garment, one cow, four goats, a pair of slippers and one umbrella. I keep count only of these. If someone steals them I would know instantly. I don't keep score of my years, who will steal them?' Bah! how cleverly the old man had tricked me. Henceforth, I too would not reveal my age.

'Whose son are you?'

'Vinasithambi,' I blurted the first name that came to my lips.

'Vinasithambi? I don't think anyone like that lives around here.' His voice sounded feeble. I was already hundred feet away, running!

It was just my luck that the rail-gate was closed. I had never travelled by train, but had heard that a train travels faster than a flying bird. At any time, one could stand gazing at it for hours. On both sides of the track, people had gathered to watch the train pass by. We heard it whistle 'coo', and in the distance where the tracks curved, a puff of smoke wisped towards the sky. The train burst into the station with the front and rear ends of each compartment rattling and shaking all over. With half the train outside the station, a solitary man stepped down from it with a huge fish secured firmly in a palmyra basket. For this single man, his fish and palmyra basket, that gigantic train had stopped at a small village station and was now preparing to leave. The smell of the train vanished and we were now engulfed by the smell of the fish.

Outside the shop next to the station, a moustached young man was sitting on a broken bench. A board above his head warned: 'Don't Spit Here.' He was probably thirty years old and was wearing a long-sleeved white shirt and a matching dhoti. A green handkerchief was tucked into his shirt collar.

103

As if someone were holding a knife to his back, he sat very erect and drank his tea. The folks who were standing around him bent down reverentially as they spoke. His attitude gave him the appearance of an emperor. I remembered that he was the local thug, Rowdy Shanmugam. After he had finished his tea, the shop owner stepped down and took the glass back.

'Cigarette!' he ordered. The owner handed him a 'Three Roses' cigarette. With the long hemp rope that was smouldering and hanging in front of the shop, he lit his cigarette and took a puff. The way he inhaled and blew out the smoke looked very stylish.

As if by magic, my schoolmate, Veerasingam, showed up at my side and gently nudged me with his elbow. 'He has committed three murders. Wait and see, today there will be one more,' he whispered.

'How do you know?'

'That's the plan they are hatching now,' he replied.

Shanmugam's unfolded left sleeve hung loose and long. Perhaps a knife was hidden there. Then the thug got up suddenly and began walking away, followed by his two sidekicks. 'This village's headcount will go down by one,' one of them said, and the other laughed. As they left, a slight breeze blew over me and made me shiver.

Veerasingam had come to the shop to rent a bicycle. He was two years older than me and had a face that looked as if he always had food inside his mouth waiting to be swallowed. He was a great runner, but he couldn't ride a bike. He was on familiar terms with the shop owner, who let him rent his bicycles. As he was forced to monkey-pedal, he had to go round in a circle before coming towards me. He held my face, turned it towards him and said: 'Why don't you try riding a cycle as well? As I don't use the seat I only have to pay half-price. You don't need to pay.'

I needed a bike that was a little smaller or legs that were a little longer. 'This is no good for me. I am getting a new one from Colombo,' I said, without batting an eyelid. Veerasingam bought my story.

Just then, a bride and groom were going to the temple with a retinue of well-wishers. The marriage ceremony must have just ended that morning. The bride looked downwards, her chin almost touching her chest. All the jewels she had worn on her hands, head and neck were glittering in the sun. Encircling her neck was a thaali, the marriage pendant. Even her braid was adorned by a long jewel. A special puja was performed for them at the temple. Someone repeatedly scaled the wall halfway and jumped down in order to ring the bell. The newlyweds and their entourage were served sweetened rice from the temple. The person who distributed it looked at me and asked, 'Are you hungry?' He didn't know that I was the guy who invented hunger. My folks had made a vow to the temple when I was born and tied a square five cent coin wrapped in a piece of cloth as a talisman around my wrist. Now I stretched out that hand with the talisman and a little bit of sweet rice plopped into my palm. I stared and there was still plenty of space left in my palm.

Suddenly, I felt a huge wave of hunger gnawing at me.

Until then I had forgotten about it. Now a fear started to grip me. If I went home late, my little brother would have finished my share of lunch. One day when I came home late, he was eating out of my plate, the one that had blue flowers painted on it. The plate with the red flowers was his.

'Why are you eating from my plate?' I asked, lurching towards him. His red plate lay unwashed right next to him. As I was late, he had almost polished off the food on my plate as well. 'Why the hell did you eat my food?' I screamed. Being a smart-ass, he replied: 'Your food? Did it have your name written on it?' I stood there dumbfounded. 'A man can wait for his food, but food cannot wait for man,' my little brother said.

The sun shone high and the street adjoining the temple glittered. Like the edges of a burning letter, the sky simmered, gathering brilliance. The treeless street stretched out emptily into the distance. Afar, a black cow was ambling forth. After a while it began to look like a man bearing something black. Only after the figure came closer did I realize that it was Lalitha, the teacher, who taught us Math at school. She was wearing slippers and was holding a black umbrella in her hand. She was approaching slowly, as if she were enjoying the scenery. Her yellow-bordered sari flapped around her legs. I liked her. Just like the eye doctor's board with big letters at the top and tiny letters at the bottom, she would start writing at the top of the blackboard in big fonts and end up in tiny ones as she neared the bottom.

Like a black and white photograph converted into colour,

she would plaster her dark face with white face powder before she entered the classroom.

'What should you do to subtract five from four?' she would ask the class.

'Don't know, teacher.'

'Can you take five from four?'

'No.'

'If you don't have enough, you have to borrow one from the next number,' she would say. My father never liked the people who came to our house to collect debts. But our teacher was telling us to borrow. I was very confused.

Looking at me under the glaring sun, she squinted a bit and asked, 'What are you doing here?' Once, when someone had died, they flew the school flag at half-mast. We were all ecstatic about the unexpected holiday. But that day I saw Lalitha teacher crying. She was very kind-hearted. She asked me again what I was doing there.

'I came to borrow the math textbook.'

'From whom?'

Two lies of equal weight popped up in my brain and I told one of them.

'Ok, Ok, you won't last in this heat, run home.'

She chased me away and walked unhurriedly, holding her umbrella at an angle.

Beneath the tamarind tree, two women jostled me and moved ahead. 'The greatest wonder in this world occurs at the moment when one life separates from another and they become two,' one of them said.

'This has been going on since the day the world began and no one considers it a miracle any more. Everyone thinks that the village headcount will increase by one,' replied the other.

I remembered what Rowdy Shanmugam's sidekick had said about the village headcount going down by one. Two people stood talking to my father beneath the tree. Father's voice was laced with laughter. From inside the house came the sound of a baby crying. The midwife fetched a basin full of dirty water and emptied it outside.

'Where the hell were you?' my father shouted. Our dog, which had been lying by my father, suddenly rose and ran away. The day's events went through my mind in reverse order. Two women, teacher, temple, newlywed couple, Veerasingam, Rowdy Shanmugam, train, old man, dog, tamarind fruit... Father was waiting for an answer. I took in a bit of air and filled my lungs. I remembered the last time my father had slapped me, his palm had left an imprint on my face. Usually several lies come out of my mouth in the space of a second. But that day, my brain came up empty. As Lalitha teacher would say, 'I had to borrow one.'

twelve

Tomorrow

SUDDENLY IN A matter of seconds there was a great commotion. 'Get up, get up,' Periyavan, the elder one, said as he hurried Chinnavan, his younger brother. It was difficult to wake Chinnavan when he was exhausted. But Periyavan did not have the heart to go away and leave his little brother sleeping there.

A few people had reported that they had seen many vehicles at a distance, driving down towards them. Further interrogation, however, had revealed that this was not a first-person account. They had just heard from others who claimed to have seen the vehicles. Nothing was certain. But that did not stop the people from running around in all directions. They formed queues at whatever spots they thought were the right ones. But soon they discovered they were in the wrong place and hurried away, only to form queues elsewhere. It was all chaos. There was much talk again of vehicles. Who saw them? Did anyone really see them coming? This was certainly not the time for playing pranks! From where were the vehicles coming? 'Take a good look, please, and tell us.'

A fat woman propelled herself forward with her four children. She had large pots in her hands. She had considered all the alternatives and had come prepared. After she had moved away, there was a gap in the line, as if a big army had marched through. Before Periyavan could run to take her place, the file had, very quickly, closed in.

Helicopters hovered above, round and round, the guns attached to them moving slowly. The rotor blades of the helicopters seemed to chant menacingly, 'Death, death...,' reminding him of the death of his parents. For a moment, Periyavan was struck by the memory of his parents, but he had no time to dwell on it, the vehicles had certainly arrived. Chinnavan ran after Periyavan, holding on to his brother's loose, torn overcoat. His face betrayed the fear that his brother might leave him behind. The mucus – which had been collecting there for the past three days – had dried up underneath his nose and was now stuck to the skin. Periyavan held on tightly to a tin can that was twisted a little out of shape from all his efforts to plug the holes in it. He was not more than eleven years old and his young brother just about six. In that vast ocean of people, the two boys were like two small leaves struggling to keep themselves afloat.

Then a dark, gigantic figure came up to them. His face proclaimed that he was used to bossing around the less fortunate. The man was in an outsized overcoat, belt and cap.

He was rolling a baton in his hands. He said something in a loud voice. Though nobody could understand what he was saying, the huge crowd guessed his commands and obeyed them.

Suddenly, a wave of people swept through that place. In the confusion, Periyavan felt his brother's hand slip from his. The crowd kept pushing him from all sides. Though he could hear Chinnavan's shouts of 'Anna, Anna', he could not turn around to see the little boy. The crowd swept him away until he could not hear Chinnavan's cries any more.

Instead of standing at the place where he had been separated from his brother, Chinnavan ran in search of his elder brother. They went in opposite directions looking for each other. An officer came by then, pulled Chinnavan out and made him stand in front of a tent. He waited there, crying, for half an hour until finally the officer came back with his brother. Chinnavan ran to his brother and hugged him. Periyavan pulled at his hair affectionately. There was a scar on his head, a big circular spot where hair had stopped growing. There were tears in Periyavan's eyes. He wiped them on his shoulders without anybody noticing it.

Several new, irregular queues formed and reformed. Periyavan ran to one of those and took his place in it. He often looked behind him to check if there were others behind him in line. He felt comforted when he saw more people join his line. They were all adults. He came up only to their waist when they were jostling each other. He tried hard not to get squashed between them.

111

Following his brother's instructions, Chinnavan was not standing in the line; he had gone to sit near the fence. Periyavan kept an eye on him and now and then shouted words of warning to him. Some other old men and young boys were resting there. Chinnavan walked all around them as if he were overseeing them. A girl was hugging a rag doll. The doll had red hair and large, black eyes. The boy went near her, eager to have a look at the doll. The girl did not like him coming near her. She moved away with her doll. He was disappointed.

The line had begun to move forward. Periyavan had told his brother that they were sure to get some meat that day. He had been deceiving the young boy for a week now, but the boy was not to be appeased any more. Periyavan thought it would be nice if they did get some meat that day. He turned to see where the line ended. He was happy that it was quite long. There were only twenty people before him; not long now before his turn came.

He noticed a sudden slight nip in the air. He hoped the wind would not get any stronger or colder. The sun had not come out at all, as if it had taken the day off. The cold wind seemed to directly attack his belly, penetrating the overcoat he held tight to his body. His shoes, with many holes, had lost their ability to keep his feet warm or protected.

A woman with a scarf tied around her head stood distributing loaves of bread, taking them one by one from a big basket. Periyavan thought that she looked a lot like his mother. Her painted fingers, too, reminded him of his mother. As she doled out the pieces of bread with a graceful movement of her hand, she kept talking to the man standing next to her, who was engrossed in doling out hot soup. Periyavan took an instant liking to her. After receiving their bread, the people took the soup in tins, plates or whatever other containers they had. Some started to sip at the soup even before they had moved out of the line.

Periyavan accepted a loaf, put it in the inner pocket of his overcoat and stretched out the tin for the soup. A moustached man asked for his registration card. He handed it over to the man. 'Hey, you! Come here. How did you get in? This card is not valid in this camp.' Periyavan moved on to the place where the soup was being served. The moustached man returned the card and said, 'I don't want to see you here again.'

Periyavan's eyes were on the man who was pouring out the soup. He keenly watched the soup to see if there were any meat pieces in it. The man in front of him had told the man serving the soup, 'Friend, please give the soup a good stir, top to bottom, before you serve it.' Periyavan, imitating the man, repeated the request. 'Sure, sure, young friend,' replied the man pleasantly. He stirred the soup well and then ladled it over. Periyavan thanked him and came out running.

He divided the bread into three parts. He hid one portion inside his coat. He gave one to his brother and took one for himself. Hungry as they were, they ate the bread in no time, dipping it into the soup. When Chinnavan saw that there was not a single piece of meat in the soup, he said, 'Brother, you cheated me; you said we would get meat today. Did we walk all those five miles for nothing? My legs are aching.'

'We have to be patient, little one. It is just that we were unlucky today. We'll definitely get some tomorrow. Don't worry.'

The sun would be out for only a couple of hours more. They needed to get back to their hide-out soon. Chinnavan came out first through the hole in the wire fence. He took off his overcoat and threw it to his brother through the hole. It cushioned the younger boy's way out.

On the highway two armed soldiers stood guard every hundred yards. The boys watched with curiosity. The soldiers stood straight with their automatic rifles. Their dress and the way they carried themselves kindled a sense of awe in the boys. One of the soldiers was light-complexioned and tall. The other was smoking a cigarette, preoccupied. The soldiers did not notice the boys until they got very close to them. One of them jumped to attention as soon as he saw the boys. The other shouted at them. The boys got scared; they did not understand what the soldier had said. His language sounded very strange and commanding, something that matched the authority of his appearance.

Periyavan put two fingers to his lips and made signs that he wanted a cigarette. After considering it for a moment, the soldier took out a cigarette from his pack and flung it on the ground. Periyavan picked it up and ran. The two boys rested a while near a bush. Periyavan lit the cigarette and took a couple of puffs. Chinnavan wanted to have a puff too. Periyavan consoled him, 'When you get to be big like me, you can smoke. But for now, be a good boy and don't smoke.' Chinnavan accepted the wisdom of his elder brother's words.

Chinnavan picked up a stick, held it straight like a gun and started marching with it. They came to the garage as it was getting dark. Chinnavan pointed to something and said, 'There, there.' It was a dog, all skin and bones. It, too, must have been a refugee, but a refugee without a registration card. It came hesitantly over to them, sniffing at the ground.

'Shall we give this dog a name?' asked Chinnavan. Periyavan replied, 'No. If we give it a name, it will become part of our family.' He took out the piece of bread from his pocket, divided it in half and gave one half to the dog. The dog limped off with the bread in its mouth.

The garage where they were hiding was a very safe place, thanks to a big lock on the outside. Periyavan went to the back of the garage and removed a plank. After they had both crawled inside, they replaced the plank. The interior of the garage had a strong stench of rags and horse sweat. It took some time for their eyes to get used to the darkness. After a bed of sorts had been made with large cartons pulled up and old blankets spread on them, Chinnavan, tired, lay down. Periyavan stashed away the other piece of bread. It would come in handy in the early hours of the morning when Chinnavan got hungry and cried for something to eat.

Periyavan sat leaning on the cartons. Suddenly, Chinnavan woke up and came crawling to him. He hugged his brother.

'Brother, my beloved brother, you will not leave me and go away, will you?' The boy sobbed.

115

Periyavan took the younger boy in his arms and held him close. 'No, my little brother, I will never leave you and go away.' The firm voice reassured Chinnavan.

Periyavan lay there for a long time without sleeping. He had to make many plans for the next day.

'We should go to Ganj camp tomorrow,' he resolved to himself.

'It is a bigger camp. And though it is ten miles away, we are sure to get some meat there.'

At least, that was what he had heard.

thirteen

Refugee Girl

THE GIRL IN THE green-yellow-white waitress uniform was a refugee. She could have been from India or Sri Lanka, or perhaps even Guyana. Not only was she dark-complexioned, with black hair and black eyes, she also wore black lipstick and nail polish. Her name must be something long, made up of a string of consonants. She had shortened it and had pinned a badge with her name, Rathna, on the right side of her dress, near the shoulder.

True to her training, she stood a little away from the tables, at just enough of a distance to be noticed by the customers, but out of their earshot. That was the rule. And there were many other rules. While placing food on the table, she should serve from the left side of the guest: Rule 12.

She had to remove leftovers from the right side of the guest: Rule 11.

While pulling out a chair to help a customer sit, she

should stand to the left of the chair: Rule 26.

A napkin folded and placed on the left side of the plate indicated that the guest had finished eating: Rule 7.

If the napkin was kept on the chair, it meant that the guest had not yet finished his meal: Rule 9.

The cutlery set at each place on the table began from the outside and as each course was served, pieces of cutlery were removed: Rule 19.

There were many more, and she knew them all by heart.

What bothered her were not the rules themselves. It was her English classes. Her teacher had said that nouns were very important. Salt, napkin, cheese, cucumber, glass, soup, olive, lettuce… but verbs were not as important at this point. All he said was that the verbs would come and join the nouns on their own at the right time, but he had not specified when and on what date they would make their appearance. Like the chants of some old prayer, she filled her single-lined notebook with nouns and committed them to memory. How were they to be used without verbs? But the teacher had said that it would happen eventually, and she had faith in him.

Her roommate scoffed at the way she learnt everything by heart. Perhaps the roommate knew a better way to learn things. After her roommate found a lover, she had started to mark the calendar with crosses. On those days, the refugee girl could not return to her room until eleven at night. The lover spoke in a voice that rattled like a tin pipe. When he stretched out his arm for a handshake, it dangled in front of the refugee girl like a bunch of grapes. She had to do the shaking. His eyes never looked straight into hers. They were always focused on some point above her right shoulder.

That day's wedding anniversary party had been arranged by one of the Canadian elite. They were so rich, it was said, that they changed their curtains every day, the bed linen twice a day and the electric bulbs eight times a day in their house.

It was well past eleven when the refugee girl came back to her room. She was paid by the hour. At weddings and birthday parties, she was extra careful. Her supervisor did not allow for mistakes. Whenever the supervisor entered the room, her black stockings pulled up tight and her arms spread like a bird preparing to take off, a certain cubic feet of air equal to her volume would be expelled from the room. No Archimedes was needed to calculate this; the girl was capable of doing it herself.

Her supervisor also sprang surprise tests on her.

'What is this called?'

'Pudding.'

The supervisor would cut a piece of the pudding and taste it. 'Now, what is this called?'

'Leftover food.'

'What do you do with it?'

'Toss it in the garbage.'

She had passed the test.

In addition to the rules in the book, her supervisor had given her some additional duties. She should interact pleasantly with the guests. She knew this one already.

She should at all times try to satisfy the guests with an

119

intuitive understanding of their needs. She knew this one too.

Never do anything that could irritate the guests. She was aware of this as well.

Since her English was not very good, she was supposed to avoid making conversation with guests. If they asked her something, she should smile. She thought this last rule was quite unnecessary since no one really understood her.

The guests at the table across from the main table looked unusual. The one who looked like the mother was young – only about thirty years old. She guessed that the father was around fifty, the son eighteen and the daughter eight. Perhaps the woman was his second wife and the son had been born to the first wife, she thought. She was clever at making such inferences.

She was in charge of their table. They were a lively bunch. They would say something, then burst into laughter every five minutes. Perhaps it was Polish that they spoke; it was full of consonants. But she could not make out if they were nouns or verbs. She wondered: what could they all have in common? Why were they all laughing so hard? But their laughter was infectious. It made laughter well up inside her too.

It was then that she saw him looking at her. Generally, no one ever seemed to see her. But this eighteen-year-old red-haired boy was looking right at her with his piercing eyes. There were many girls at the party, but he was looking only at her. What did the rules say about this? What would her supervisor say? Could she return his gaze? She was not sure. She concentrated on her work.

She felt unnerved by this new experience. The red-haired boy turned to his sister and laughed often, saying something to her. But the remnants of his laughter were always directed towards her, the refugee girl. Every time she went to their table to serve, his eyes touched her and stayed with her until she left the room.

At one point, the napkin on his lap slipped down. She thought that his fingers might have helped accomplish that. There was a rule she had to follow; she bent down, picked up the napkin and handed it to him. He thanked her and took it from her. Even as his lips were thanking her, his fingers were, without any doubt, pressing her palm. She began to shiver right from her feet – as it always happened when she was confronted with the unfamiliar. But she quickly moved over to her place as though nothing had happened. Afraid of disturbing the air around her, she stood perfectly still. She stood at such a distance that she could not hear the guests, but could be seen by them. Rule 17.

The guests then began to dance. The boy's mother and father went to the dance floor. The mother went twirling round and round as she danced. The father, with a minimum of movements, accomplished his part. His sister turned her chair around and watched the dancers intently.

Suddenly, a smile appeared on the boy's face. He raised his hand and beckoned her. She hurried up to him and bent her wasp-like waist as much as she could, and said, 'Yes?' She was allowed to speak that much.

He said, 'Coffee, decaf, two sugars.' His words fell sweetly on her ears. It felt like he had uttered her name with love. 'Coffee, decaf, two sugars' had rolled out of his mouth so smoothly. He ordered coffee three times before the party was over. Her duty was to serve him whatever he ordered. Rule 22. She was ready to serve him even if he repeated his order twenty times.

The guests began to leave one by one. The family would also be gone soon. His mother opened her handbag, set something right in it and then slung the bag on her shoulder, getting ready to leave. The red-haired boy picked up his napkin, folded it into a square and placed it on his plate, with his eyes all the while on her.

She had managed not to violate any of the rules. She took her time piling up the cups one over another. He kept staring at her. She picked up his plate and took it inside. When she removed the napkin, a five-dollar note fell from the plate, with a phone number written in ink on the napkin. Quickly, she wrote down the number on her palm. For the second time that day, her palm came in handy.

Her roommate was not in when she got home. She turned her hand over and looked at her palm. The number was still there. She said the digits once out loud. Even the digits sounded sweet. Her mind wandered like never before. What would the red-haired boy be doing now? Would he be thinking of her? The room was silent. She thought she should call him now. She thought that nobody would answer her call at that hour. So she slowly dialled the number.

A voice spoke at the other end. She recognized the voice.

It was the same rounded voice that had said, 'Coffee, decaf two sugars.' But her hands shook, her voice faltered and her thighs trembled. She put the phone down. But exactly a minute later the phone rang. He must have dialled the last number received on his phone. She did not take the call. She stood some distance away and looked at the phone like it was a coiled snake. It continued to ring. Finally it fell silent. He had left a message.

When she replayed his message and listened to it, she could understand only half of it. His voice sounded somewhat hesitant, as if he wondered if he was speaking to the right person. But he seemed to have guessed who his caller had been. He begged her to call him again. She did not, but she played his message over and over whenever she wanted to hear his voice. It became her special ritual. Somehow, her roommate got wind of it. Perhaps she was even a trifle jealous of it. One day, her roommate erased the message when she was away. The refugee girl was in agony.

The room they shared had just a ceiling, a door and a window. Her friend's cot was right beside hers. If she stretched her hand, it would hit the other girl's face. So the refugee girl always lay very close to the wall. There were other problems as well. She did not like the way the croaky-voiced boyfriend looked at her. When her friend was not home, he would call and make enquiries about his lover. Shouldn't he hang up as soon as he was told that the girl was not available? He didn't. He would try and start a conversation with the refugee girl.

One winter day, when the sun refused to come any higher

than one's shoulder, her roommate and her boyfriend treated her to lunch. They wouldn't take 'no' for an answer. Unaware of their intentions, she went out with them. Only later did she realize that their sole aim was to torture her. They had worn dark glasses, hoisted over their foreheads as if to suggest they belonged to a particular group of elite. They often conversed in their own kind of sign language and the pair broke out in sudden bouts of loud laughter. The refugee girl had no clue what was going on, but she felt that most of their laughter was at her expense. She did not like it.

When she finally got to her workplace, she had only a few minutes left to get ready for work. Usually, she was ready and in her uniform well ahead of time. That was as per Rule 16. She could be sent to any of the dining halls. Rule 18. Some girls who had come looking for a waitress's job like hers were already there, waiting. That day she worked for ten hours, as if she were out to avenge somebody. She did not sit down even for a minute. Her legs ached. Her arms were tired from carrying heavy plates. Still she was used to that kind of work. The party went on past midnight. On such occasions the supervisor became the epitome of kindness. She'd give them a five-minute break.

There was a small room tucked in between the dining room and the party hall. It had an old-fashioned black telephone, with numbers that could be dialled. Every time she went past that contraption, she felt a great emotional turmoil. Her heart beat fast. The red haired boy came up in her thoughts that day like never before.

124

After she had called him for the first time a few weeks ago, she had called him three more times. Every time the phone was answered by a gruff male voice. Perhaps it was his father. Each time she hung up at once. But on that particular day she was desperate to hear his voice. She placed the plate she had in her hand on the floor and dialled the number on the telephone. Her fingers trembled. Her heart throbbed inside her like a sparrow in its last few moments of life.

Surprisingly, it was he who answered. She had no doubt about it. The world seemed to dry up instantly. No sound came out of her. He kept calling, 'Hello!' 'Hello!!' What was she to say? What could she say? What should be the word to speak? What should be her tone? She had not considered any of these. She had just wanted to hear his voice. He said, 'Hello!' once more.

'Mozzarella salad.'

'Lettuce.'

'Fruit cake.'

'Spaghetti vongole.'

'Lasagne.'

She did not have any verbs. She merely recited all the items the party had ordered a few weeks earlier. She only heard a faint sound, between spurts of laughter, from the other end. With that the girl hung up.

Three days later, she stretched out her legs on the bed, crossed them one over the other and tried to recall the face of the red-haired boy. Unexpectedly her friend opened the door and entered the room. The noise of her opening the door was louder than when she banged it shut; it was a wonder how she managed that. She shook off her shoes, still standing, and threw aside her handbag. Her quivering lips went up and down like eyelids, but no sound came out of her.

The refugee girl did not open her mouth. As if she had woken up just then, she rolled over to the other side and looked around. Unattractive room, bad friend, dirty blanket, and an awful smell. In the room she could see a wall no matter which way she turned. She closed her eyes once more and tried to recall his face. She remembered how his lips rolled and the words slipped off them: 'Coffee, decaf, two sugars!'

'Coffee, decaf, two sugars!'

She drifted off to sleep.

But sleep didn't come easily to the red-haired boy after she hung up on him again. It took him no time to guess it was the waitress who had rattled off all the items he had eaten at the party. It took some time for him to find out the company she worked for and when and where the company sent its employees. He kept up his efforts relentlessly. He went to different party venues and looked for her. But the refugee girl was quite unaware of all this.

Then he found her. He was at the top of the stairs. The refugee girl was standing at the bottom, holding a plate. She saw him before he saw her. The way he looked at her seemed to carry all the words that he had brought with him from Poland. Her look too conveyed nouns, verbs and all kinds of words mentioned in the grammar book. She held the plate close to her green, yellow and white chest. She looked like an angel in that uniform. He took two steps at a time and hurried towards her, only to find the plate between them. She was still holding on to it tightly. She looked down. On that plate were all kinds of food that would be eaten by some guest at that party. She broke Rules 27, 32 and 13, all at the same time.

fourteen

Dilemma

IT WAS IN DESPERATE times – when nothing was left in the house to sell – that Papa, or 'crooked brain' as he was called by his wife, had no choice but to offer up his son into a kind of servitude. The practice was called pledging and it was common in some poor villages in African nations. The son's name was Ukko. In this part of the country, the rains came by the end of April. And it was at this time of the year that his father offered him into service. Once pledged, Ukko would have to work for three or four months before he could be redeemed. So Ukko stuffed his few clothes – only a pair of pants and a shirt he wore to school – into a plastic bag. He filled the remaining space with his books. Whatever happened to him, he was not going to give up on his studies.

Despite his occasional absences, he always stood first in his class. When the boy went missing from school, his headmaster knew that he had been pledged to work somewhere. He loved the boy. When Ukko was eleven, he had come first in an examination held for all the students in that region, and the headmaster had presented him with a wristwatch. It had two hands that went round and round to show the time. Until then, Ukko had worn only toy watches whose hands you had to set manually. But this was different; the big and little hands kept going after each other all by themselves. Ukko got to wear the watch on his wrist just for one day before his Papa took it away and sold it in the market. Mama cursed him and called him 'crooked brain'! The name stuck. Ukko had three mothers, four grandmothers and one father. His mother was the second wife and all three wives had children, but when it came to the matter of pledging, his father chose only to pledge Ukko. Mama once asked Papa why he always pledged Ukko and not the other children. His reply was somewhat strange. He had said, 'I know what I am doing; you keep quiet. No matter how long he is pledged for, he will never give up on his studies and will always come first.'

This made Ukko feel proud of himself. He had on many occasions pleaded with Mama, 'I feel ashamed to see Papa drunk and engaging in street brawls. My friends make fun of me. Why don't you do something to make him mend his ways?'

Mama would laugh. 'The prayers of chickens never stopped the kites. You are a little boy,' she would say.

The first time he was pledged, he was only eleven years old. Papa left him with Lebanese businessmen. When war broke out in Lebanon, many Lebanese business people migrated to

Africa. They set up businesses and ran them profitably. They lived in luxury, owning big houses, with some six or seven servants to attend on them. Ukko was allowed to enter those houses only through the back doors. His first duty in the morning was to polish and shine his master's shoes. Then he had to clean the rooms, but he couldn't use the broom, for the Lebanese people believed that ghosts would descend on the house if they let a young boy sweep the floor. So he had to pick the rubbish off the floor with his hands. If it was a good day for his master, then it was a good day for him, but if the day turned out to be bad for the master, then it certainly would be a very bad day for Ukko, too. In the photograph hanging in the sitting room, his master stood with a gun in his right hand and his left foot on a dead deer. The animal's eyes were open. The master's eyes were also open. Looking at this photo, Ukko felt that if the master ever lifted his foot off the animal, it would run away.

Ukko was served three meals a day on aluminium plates. That kept him happy, but he could not help crying at night, thinking of his mother. In the following year, he was pledged to a Lebanese man who owned a pharmacy. There he had to work ten hours a day. His boss was tall and had a protruding belly; he wore a long robe to cover that. It was rumoured that he got his robes sewed with the front longer than the back so they would be of equal length at the front and back. Within a week, Ukko had committed to his memory all the details about the different medicines, their names, for what diseases they were prescribed, their side-effects, sale prices and so on. He would patiently explain to the customer the way a particular medicine should be taken. More than anything else, he had to remember to tell the patients that medicines once sold should never be brought back. That was the owner's rule. Since he faithfully obeyed all the orders given to him, the owner began to take a liking to him. Ukko was not paid any wages. As agreed with his father, he would only be given a place to stay in and three meals a day. However, the owner had promised him a stipend when he completed his contract and went home. But one foolish act committed by him spoiled everything.

Once every six months the pharmacy was in the habit of stacking all the medicines that had expired in cartons and taking them to the office of the Health Minister. For a substantial bribe, the minister would issue a letter extending their expiry date by one more year. Ukko, however, was not happy selling medicines past their expiry date. One day a patient with a severe breathing problem came asking for a medicine, but the stock they had was past its expiry date. If he did not sell the medicine, his master would get angry. But if he did sell the medicine, the patient would not be helped. Ukko had devised his own arbitrary way of making decisions in such tricky situations. He would count up to twenty; if a new customer entered the shop within that time, he would sell the medicine. If no one came within the stipulated time, he would not sell it. He counted rather fast and no one entered the shop, so he told the customer that the medicine was out of stock and sent him away. His boss somehow found out what he had done and yelled at him. A few days later, when Ukko's father came to redeem him, the pharmacy owner complained to him that he had incurred great losses because of the boy. He told the father sternly that Ukko was 'never to be returned', as if the boy was himself a medicine, and drove them away.

When Ukko was fifteen years old, his crooked-brained father pledged him to Balthazar's house. The new master was a prosperous diamond merchant. Like a praying mantis, he rubbed his palms together when he spoke. But he was, indeed, a man of few words. You could stand by his side for a whole day, and he would say only four or five words. Ukko had never seen such a big house in his life. The house was surrounded by a lawn and a garden, which was the size of a football field. There were a couple of black-and-white storks in the garden. They roamed the area with their red beaks held high. This master was a good man. He bought Ukko a new shirt and a pair of new shoes. The servants of the house were expected to walk around only in clean clothes. Merchants would begin to stream in right from eight in the morning. Besides coffee in small cups, they had to be served snacks like mezze, hummus and baklava. Alcoholic drinks were reserved for the evenings. Only three people lived in that house, yet there were seventeen servants working for them, including Ukko.

Ukko stood in utter shock the first day he saw Juliana, the master's daughter. He had seen many beautiful girls in the other houses where he had worked, but he had never

ever thought that such a beauty as Juliana could exist in this world. Hers was a beauty that could not be surpassed, he decided. When she pulled her beautiful hair back and tied it up in a high bun, she looked taller. Of the twenty rooms in the house, he never knew which one she was in. She was seen only rarely. One day when he was running between the kitchen and the drawing room, he came face to face with her, and her face gave him the jitters. He flinched when he tried to raise his eyes to look at her. That was when he realized that beauty could also be terrifying. She called out 'Ukko!' He was surprised that she even remembered his name, and was very proud. The day he had begun to work there, he had been told that he had to call the boss, 'master', his wife, 'madam' and his daughter, 'little madam'.

So he said, 'Yes, little madam,' with head bowed down. His eyes saw only her sandals, which were decorated with silver lace. His close-fitting shirt was half drenched in sweat. 'I heard that you go to school. What do you study?' she asked. He racked his brain for an answer. A few days ago, he had seen the books that were strewn on the table. She must have been a couple of years older than him, but she was in a lower class, one year junior to him. She stood there, hands on her hips, waiting for an answer. She might have wondered why he took so long to answer such a simple question. She was in a light green dress with a white collar. She also had a broad belt, as white as her collar, tied tightly around her waist. Wisely, he mentioned a class lower to the one he really was in. 'Okay, you may go,' she said. As she said this, her head tilted at a forty degree angle towards her shoulder. He walked away feeling like he had been released from an impending calamity. But the moment he left her presence, a deep sense of loss engulfed him. He was in hell for the rest of the day.

His mother had protested when his crooked-brained Papa had decided to pledge him that year. She was bedridden then and was being looked after by his stepmother, his father's third wife. No one else ever came near her. The doctors had given up all hope. Writhing in pain, she would moan, 'Why should I have this disease which I cannot even pronounce?'

She would call out 'Ukko, Ukko' four times in a minute. He did not have to do anything but go and sit beside her. The flies seemed to bother her a lot. They attacked her eyes all the time. In a rich man's house, there were no flies at all. He could not understand how these flies knew the difference between a rich house and a poor one. For the first time in his life, he hated himself for his helplessness. Usually, he eagerly awaited the day when his crooked-brained Papa would come and release him from the bondage. But this time, having seen the girl, he worried that his father might come and release him too soon. This thought made him feel ashamed.

There were only two souls in the entire world who loved him. One was his Mama and the other the headmaster of his school. The headmaster would spread out the map of England before Ukko and say, 'You are a good, hard-working boy, and you are very intelligent. You should go abroad for university.' The boy would start sobbing. Annoyed at this outburst, the headmaster would say, 'You are the only one in this world who cries at the very sight of a map,' and he would put away the map. Ukko was unable to bear the sight of it.

'I'll not go anywhere outside this country, sir,' he would moan.

'Your brain works like a pendulum,' the older man would counsel. 'You appear to be a very intelligent boy one moment, but the next moment you behave like the stupidest child on earth. The bird that does not leave its branch will not know where the worm is. You should be like the bee that seeks out honey by going from flower to flower. Go all over seeking knowledge.' Ukko would hang his head.

One day at Balthazar's house, the doorbell rang. Before the sound had died, it rang again. Ukko ran to the door and opened it. There were two young girls at the door, standing so close to each other that it seemed as if their shoulders were locked together. Ukko smiled at them. But the girls did not return the smile. They came in almost knocking him down. He understood that they were Juliana's classmates. One held a ladle – pretending it was a microphone – in front of her mouth and began to sing. The other girl danced to that song in the middle of that lounge. He later found out that it was an Arabic dance. It seemed she had learnt an Arabic dance from a teacher. Then came Juliana's turn. She had tied blue and red ribbons around her waist, making it seem even smaller than usual, and danced. The main movement of her dance was to shake her hips and pirouette. She stood with one leg straight and the other bent, with a hand on her hip, and she kept raising and flinging out her hips at regular intervals. Only her hips went up and down. When he went in to serve them mezze, the girl with the ladle hid it behind her. But she could not hide her mouth. As he turned to leave the room, Juliana said something softly to them, and they both turned their heads at the same time to look at him. That made him self-conscious and shy. Even after he had run into the kitchen, his thighs were shaking. All night, he wondered what Juliana could have told her friends.

Juliana had innumerable clothes. Pajamas and casual wear, school uniform, sports clothes, bathing suits, outdoor dresses, party dresses, and so on. In fact, he never saw her wear the same dress twice. Sometimes she would wear a party dress at home and spend hours looking at herself in the mirror. In a long light blue dress that flowed behind her, she would tap her high-heeled shoes noisily on the floor, looking like a princess. She would change her clothes many times in a day. The discarded dress would remain in the very place she had dropped it, forming a circle on the floor. Ukko had, on many occasions, picked up the dresses and dropped them in the laundry basket. The few seconds that it took to feel the softness of those clothes stayed with him for hours. He would pick them up with great respect, as if he was actually touching the girl herself.

Gardeners mowed the lawn regularly, raising a huge din. On those grass-mowing days, he would not hear Juliana calling him. She might call him from any of the twenty rooms in the house. Her voice would echo through the different walls and by the time it reached him, it would have lost its initial strength. But he would go searching for her from room to room. That day, she was concentrating on some lesson. It seemed as though she was doing her homework. He took a sly peep into her book. It was a problem about Pascal's triangle. 'Yes, little madam,' he said. She asked him to bring her some tea. He went down the stairs, fetched a cup of tea from the kitchen and handed it to her as if he were offering her a bouquet of flowers. Even after she had taken the cup from him, he kept his hand outstretched. She said it had become cold. He ran again to the kitchen and brought her another cup of tea. That, too, was not to her liking. The third time he took the steps two at a time and came back with her tea, breathing heavily like a race horse. She said, 'Mm, it is cold.' She had not even touched the cup. He said, 'Small madam, you seem to be angry with me over something?'

'Me? Angry? With you? Go, go away,' she drove him away with her hands. He staggered as he walked back and fell down, spilling the tea all over himself. She did not expect this. She ran up to him, gave him a hand to get up and said, 'Oh, I'm sorry.'

He felt the soft fingers for just a moment, but the thrill of her touch stayed with him for a long time. The sun's rays pierced the room through the window. The sound of the lawnmowers seemed to amplify and envelop them. Since then, and for the rest of his life, every time he heard a lawnmower he would think of her.

His mind had become obsessed with her. He went round the whole day keeping her in sight. His legs took on a new speed. One day, rather strangely, Juliana put her arms around her mother's neck like a coiling snake and said something in Arabic. Then it looked as if she turned her head towards where he was. He was afraid that she would vanish if he even blinked. The next day when she left for school, he stood in front of the house on the pretext of having some work to do. He could not be sure if she turned to look at him before she got into the car. Again in the evening he calculated the hour of her return from school and waited. But to his shock, his crooked-brain Papa showed up, released him and took him home.

In that year's public examinations, he came first in the country. His headmaster told him that the British Council had offered him a scholarship to continue his studies in England. All he could say was, 'For me?' His eyes began to well up. He came home panting and gave his mother the news. As soon as he had spoken, he realized his folly. For the past six months, she had been confined to her bed. Groaning in pain, she stroked his head and merely said, 'So, you are going to leave me?' She did not say anything after that. Mama knew three languages. Her village dialect Fulani, the Timni language she used when she spoke to his crooked-brained Papa, and Creole. But in the subsequent days Mama chose to remain silent in all three languages.

Papa ordered him to go to the market bus stand and fetch his second grandmother. She would cheer up Mama. It was in the morning hours when the harmattan winds blew over them. The breeze brought the cold with it from the Sahara.

When he breathed, misty clouds that looked like his lungs floated ahead of him. He had not been told at what time and by which bus grandmother would arrive. He searched every bus that came. Ahead of him, a woman was also waiting for somebody. She had tied a baby to her back and was carrying another baby in a bucket. Buses came and went. Reading the messages written on those buses, he waited for his grandmother. Some lines were funny. 'Any child, not sitting on the lap, will be charged full fare.' 'God is up there; if you are in a hurry to meet him, take the next bus.' 'It is illegal to carry corpses.'

Then suddenly, as if a bright light had been directed at his eyes, he was blinded by shock. His heart skipped a beat. He saw Juliana with her two friends who had never returned his smiles. As she walked on the other side of the road, her dazzling dress swirled around her in keeping with her steps. Ukko looked down at what he was wearing. Tight khaki shorts and a dirty grey shirt that he had been wearing that whole week. Just like a guinea fowl hiding its head inside a bush, he moved slowly backwards and hid himself behind a bus. She walked away laughing and talking with her friends, free of any worry. As soon as her form disappeared from his view, he yearned to look at her once more. What a walk she had! As if she orchestrated all movements of the universe! Such grace! She turned her head towards her friends and said something. With just the same suddenness with which she had appeared, she disappeared. He never saw her again.

The headmaster came to his home looking for him. He

was very angry. 'Is it true? You are not going? Do you know you have brought your village glory and fame?'

Ukko spoke, looking at the floor: 'Mama does not like it, sir.'

'What are you talking about? Here I am pointing out the moon to you; and you see only the tip of my finger! Your grandma is here to take care of your Mama.' The headmaster spoke to him for quite a while that day. 'Everything is ready. All you have to do is go to the capital city tomorrow.'

'But I can't, sir,' Ukko said.

'The door is wide open, but you are looking through the keyhole,' the headmaster said and went off in a huff. Ukko had never before seen him so angry.

Mama was staring at her son. She said, 'I'll die soon.'

'I'll never leave you, Mama,' he said and hugged her. Her body smelled of dying skin.

He hadn't slept three nights in a row. But that night, when he woke up by chance at midnight, somebody was stroking his forehead. He opened his eyes and found Mama by his side. Her fingers on his forehead were like sticks of ginger pulled out freshly from the soil. Her lips were white. Was she the woman who had once suckled and reared him? When he touched her shoulder, it was sharp as a knife. All the teeth in her mouth looked huge in the faint light thrown by the oil lamp, and it scared him. 'What is it, Mama? You are not able to sleep?' he asked her.

'If I sleep, you will leave me and go away,' she said.

'No, Mama! I will never go,' he promised her and gave

her some sleeping tablets. She took them and went to sleep peacefully.

When he left his house at five in the morning, his mother was in a deep sleep. He picked up his bag. He had never ever lied to his mother before. He could not imagine how much she would suffer when she got to know that he was gone. There was no one at the bus stop except a stray dog. His mind wavered; he was not sure if he should go back home. He thought of how his headmaster had left his house in anger. But he had only one mother. If his studies got interrupted now, he could always take up another course of study later on. But where would he find another mother! When he thought that he might never ever see her again, he trembled. But that thought was pushed aside by another image. Her nails shining like the inside of a sea-shell, head tilted to one side, Juliana was laughing gently. He was taken aback by this sudden vision.

He looked at the dog. It looked back at him without lifting its head, through the top of its eyes. The bus would be there in another few minutes. If the dog got up and left the place before the bus arrived, he would go back home. But if the dog stayed there, he would take the bus. It was a sign and he decided to follow it. In that manner the matter that had troubled him for four days was resolved.

fifteen

The Five-legged Man

THE WOMAN CAME and sat down heavily by my side on
one of the benches outside the supermarket. She was in
her work clothes and had a paper cup of coffee in her hand. It
was clear that she was a cleaning woman taking a break. She
looked about fifty. She had black hair, blue eyes and light skin.
I guessed that she was perhaps Eastern European or Russian.
She drank her coffee silently, and her thoughts seemed to be
somewhere else. I hadn't seen so much sadness in anyone's
eyes ever. That's why I decided to strike up a conversation
with her.

'So are you done for the day?' I said.

'No, not yet, only done with half my work. I am just taking
a break,' she said. From her clothes, make-up, speech and
demeanour, I guessed that she had been in Toronto for quite
some time. Usually, those who worked as cleaners were more
than likely to be new arrivals to Canada, or those who had

come here seeking a refugee status. Most of them changed to other jobs once they had been in the country for a while. That's why I was so surprised at seeing a long-time immigrant still working as a cleaning woman.

'When did you migrate to Canada?' I asked her.

She was Greek. She'd come to Canada by herself when was only thirteen years old. Her father had named her 'Helen' after Helen of Troy in Homer's epic literary work. Famous for her great beauty, the mythological Helen was abducted and carried across the seas by the great warrior Paris. This contemporary Helen, too, had met with a more or less similar fate. Here is the rest of her story, as she told it to me.

'We were seven children; I was the sixth. Though my father had only one leg, he was always seen astride a horse. You could see him on his saddle at all hours, except when he went to sleep. His job was to take the nobles on hunting expeditions. He was a good hunter himself, quite adept at shooting, and never missed his target. His knowledge of the forest too was good. Only he knew where and when certain birds and animals could be found. So the elite sought him out. If the booty was large, father got more money than initially agreed upon.

In the years after I was born, there was a decline in hunting as a sport. Gradually, my father's earnings dwindled. He did not have any other skills. So he would continue to take hunters out to shoot. In fact, he spent so much time on the horse that he was known in our village as the five-legged man. By the time I was about eleven or twelve, things got worse; we had to go without food for many days. But father was continuously trying to find some way of supporting his family.

'I was a good student and was keen on continuing my studies. The Greek epics attracted me a great deal. I was also interested in learning the ancient classical language. Modern Greek is very different from its earlier form. Though the script is the same, ancient Greek pronunciation and the meanings are very different.

'My mother's sister, who lived a life of comfort in Canada, invited me to come and stay with her. She tempted me, saying that once I got here I could study whatever I wished. I jumped with joy. Even amidst such poverty, even though my departure would definitely help them, my mother was not happy about my leaving them. But my father thought it was a great honour and was immensely proud of me. He went around the village on his horse at least four times to announce the news that I was going to Canada for higher education. I arrived in Montreal in December 1969, in the beginning of winter. My aunt had two children. The day I arrived I was allowed to sleep in their room. They slept on cots; I slept on the floor. But the next morning reality hit me: I had been brought here to be my aunt's unpaid servant.

'We have a story in Greek mythology about the king of Troy, who planned to raise a huge wall around his city. He appointed the inimitable warrior, Apollo, and the sea god, Poseidon, to do the work. He had promised them suitable rewards after they finished building the wall. But once the wall was up, he cheated them and didn't give them their money. This king was the worst of all the conmen in Greek mythology. My aunt was a good match for him. With a well-planned trick, she had conned me. After she went off to work in the mornings, I had to take care of her two children, and also cook, wash and clean the house. When I asked her about my schooling, she said I had to wait for the winter to be over. New enrolment would take place in September. But it was an excuse and every month, she just thought of new excuses. She never sent me to school.

'She made me tear up the letters that I wrote home and made me rewrite them. She would then take the letter, put it inside an envelope and post it. Morning, noon, evening and night blurred together. I never left the house. I did not learn any French either. In short, I led the life of a slave. But back home, my father was under the happy impression that I was getting a higher education. I did not know what my aunt wrote in the letters she sent him. My father never failed to write back, "Study hard; you should come first in the next exam as well."

'My birthdays came and went. Only I kept count of them. No one ever sang "Happy Birthday" for me. One day after they had all gone to bed, I stood in front of the mirror and took a good look at myself. I was surprised to see a young teenager's reflection in the mirror. I stood there for quite some time, looking at my image. She had slapped me because I had left the carpet half rolled up and forgotten to unroll it after I had finished the cleaning. As I looked in the mirror the slap appeared to be on the opposite side of my face. My condition made me wallow in self-pity.

'My aunt had an invaluable antique piece, a crystal glass candelabrum with seven branches. Once, while I was cleaning, it slipped from my hand, fell and broke. The sound of breaking glass brought my aunt from somewhere inside the house, a hand raised to strike, shouting, "You devil! You have broken it?" I do not know what happened to me that day, but suddenly I was so enraged that I stood up to her. No longer a child, I was an eighteen-year-old young woman. I faced her straight with hands on my hips and asked, "So what?" She stood there transfixed. For the first time I saw panic on her face. She moved slowly backwards like a photographer planning to take a snapshot. She picked up the young baby playing on the floor and went out of the room. I did not sweep away the glass pieces that day. I just went to bed. That was the longest night of my life. The next morning I stole the money needed for my bus fare and took the bus to Toronto.'

'Were you happy in Toronto?'

'The day I arrived in Toronto was the first day of spring. The sky looked as if it was within arm's reach. The trees were all in bud, indicating the beginnings of a new life. I was very happy. I got a job in a garment factory, sewing buttons. I felt liberated; I married a co-worker; I had a son. Life was good. Then, all of a sudden, my husband came up with this idea of opening a restaurant. We scraped together all our savings and set up a Greek eatery. It began making a profit after a few years. But later when my husband died, I had to sell it at a loss.'

146

'Did you ever meet your aunt after that?'

'The day I first came to Montreal, my aunt sort of felt my pulse, looked at me from all angles. I thought she was expressing her love for me, but I was wrong. I now feel that she was only trying to decide how much I was worth. Her only concern was how much work she could extract from me. Of all the cruel things she said, I remember one the most. "Why is it that you are so hell-bent on getting an education? You look quite pretty with the broom in your hand." That was my aunt. Until the day he died, my father did not know that he had been deceived. Mama heard about it when I wrote to her after I came to Toronto. Mama never forgave my aunt, but I have, though the hurt she caused me is still very raw. There is a proverb in our country: one who sells shoes has no choice but to go down on her knees. Once my aunt had made me her housemaid, could I ever disobey her? She thought she was a great beauty, but she was not. She looked bloated, like she had been soaked in water. But she was a very hard taskmaster. Her eyes always darted from place to place, like those of an insect. And her favourite pastime was to find fault with my work. Any lapse would bring on a stream of abuse from her. She usually spoke to me in Greek, but when she had to scold me she would switch over to English. That was how I learnt my English.'

I asked her, 'You have a son?'

'I thought my son would get the higher education I had dreamed of, but he did not even finish high school. Without my knowledge, he married a girl he'd known only for ten days. Whenever that girl laughed, cigarette smoke came out of her mouth. He ran away with her to Idaho, in the US. If anyone learns of the reason that he gave me for moving there, they'd laugh. He said he would be able to shoot ducks there. I am told it is the state where the writer Ernest Hemmingway shot ducks! Am I not worth as much as a duck? Is this a good reason for a son to abandon his mother? He doesn't even stay in touch. I have nobody and I live alone. I think of my father often. He never stopped working until his last day. When people of his town made fun of him as the "five-legged man", he never paid any attention to them. One day he died seated on his horse. He laboured tirelessly until his death, with just one leg. And I have got two!' she laughed.

The woman with the beautiful name, Helen, got up suddenly, shook her dress and straightened it. Looking at her again, I thought she must have been a great beauty once. She threw her coffee cup into the waste bin that she had cleaned just a while ago. And set out, pushing her cart filled with brooms, a bucket of soapy water and antiseptic lotion. Her very last words: 'I picked up the broom when I was thirteen to sweep and clean. Today, at fifty-five, I am still doing the same, and perhaps doing it less well.'

I thought to myself her words were a perfect closing line for a short story.

sixteen

The Girl on the Train

HIS FIRST PROBLEM WITH Canada was that winter came every year. Everything he wore – jacket, shirt, shoes – was cheap. He shivered, even on the subway. Now, for the third time, he was going to meet the lawyer who was handling his refugee claim. He had told this lawyer the truth about what had happened to him. After insisting that his story was unconvincing, the lawyer created another story based on already existing evidence to support his case. It was this story that the court had rejected.

About twenty minutes away from his stop, a girl got on the train. His legs shook uncontrollably from the moment he spotted her. The sound of his heart beating seemed louder in his ears than the sound of the train. Like him, she was neither fair nor dark. She wore a soft jacket and warm boots. She looked at him pointedly for a mere second, before retrieving a book from her bag. It looked like a textbook. She got off at the next station, but his heart continued to race. In that instant he decided that if he were ever to take his life, it would be by throwing himself under a train in which she was travelling.

Whenever he thought of suicide, he also thought of the Somali. It was the Somali who saved him from dying of starvation in the Milan Central Station in Italy. Because the Somali had travelled to so many countries, he had worked out the ideal mode of suicide suitable for each country. Poison in Belgium, gunshot in Italy, and in Paris, naturally, the Eiffel Tower. In Venice, one didn't have to bother since the city itself was gradually sinking in water. He never knew what became of the Somali.

The year he had left Colombo alone and arrived in Rome, they had said that winter could arrive at any time. That year remained etched in his memory. It was the year that the President of Sri Lanka, Ranasinghe Premadasa, was assassinated. His trip to Rome was arranged by an 'uncle' who scraped the money together. His uncle, who always forgot his name, told him to proceed directly to Greece and then board a ship. It seemed like a simple, straightforward plan. Since he had a perfectly forged visa to Greece, he didn't foresee any problems. How was he to know that even after three years he would never find that ship?

The officer who apprehended him at the border in Greece was tall and thin and wore a white uniform. As he flipped through the passport, he rearranged his face. Strongly resembling an angry, salivating beast, the officer yelled loudly at him. His voice was ten times his size and his teeth shook as the words poured from his lips. His abuse was incomprehensible, like the saying, 'It was all Greek to me.' Later, the officer put him on a train to Venice and told him never to come back. Halfway through, when the ticket inspector confronted him, he translated one by one the Tamil words into whatever English words he knew and pleaded for mercy. The ticket inspector was unmoved and fined him an equivalent of 50 dollars. It was an enormous sum, but he paid up as he had no choice. He realized that a language is useful only to the extent that it is understood by someone else. Otherwise, whether you know a language or not makes no difference.

When he got off at the station in Venice, he was a little surprised that in the midst of all his grief there was a grain of joy. He had read the *Merchant of Venice* in Tamil and now as he looked at that city, he was in complete awe. He remembered Shakespeare's Bassanio, his lover, Portia, and the devoted friend, Antonio, who agreed to stand surety for 3000 ducats. When he thought of Shylock, he wondered what a shop would look like in Venice and he opened the door of a nearby store to peer inside. The door opened with a chime. A girl came rushing out, yelling, 'Go! Go!' and when he hastily retreated, the door closed again with a chime. It reminded him of the abuse Shylock must have taken on those streets. He was struck by the wisdom of Shylock's words, 'I am a Jew. If you prick us, do we not bleed? If you tickle us, do we not laugh? If you poison us, do we not die?' How much did the people of this beautiful city hate outsiders? It seemed that the city had not changed much since the time when Shakespeare had described it. He went back to the Santa Lucia Station and sat down on a bench. It was then that the Somali, wafting towards him gently like a falling leaf, appeared and sat next to him. 'Refugee! What's your name?' the Somali asked. 'Mahesh,' he replied.

Mahesh worked in a furniture factory in Toronto. In the morning, he got his instructions for the day. He was given details on how many planks were required, their length, width and thickness. For the whole day, wearing a mask and gloves, his job was to saw timber to the given specifications. And during this entire time, he thought about her – the girl on the train. What was the point in thinking about a girl he had seen only once? But it was like listening to a song; when his thoughts were on her, he hardly felt the day going by.

The following week he did not see her. He always got on to the same train at the same time. Then one day, without warning, she appeared. As all the seats in the compartment were taken, she held on to the bar overhead, swaying ever so slightly with the movement of the train. Her eyes had the startled look of someone who had just received some unexpected news. She could have been from India, Sri Lanka, or Guyana. The light bounced off her slightly pouting lips, making her even more alluring. She moved briskly when the train stopped and in a fleeting moment, her clothes seemed to twirl, detach themselves, and then follow her. If only she had glanced back just once, it would have been so comforting.

After arriving in Canada, Mahesh had thought of suicide a few times. Although it was a foregone conclusion that he would end his life by throwing himself under a subway train, the specific train and time were determined only after he saw the girl. He was contemplating suicide on the day his refugee claim was denied, but his lawyer stopped him with the prospect of a successful appeal. The first time he had serious thoughts of suicide was when his seventh interview for a job failed. His first interview was quite funny. The employer sat on his high chair and asked questions: 'Did you fill out this form by yourself?'

'Yes, I did. I did.'

'Do you own the clothes you are wearing?'

The official had somehow figured out that they were borrowed clothes.

'Yes, these clothes are for me. For me only.'

'Is the photograph on the application yours?'

'Yes, it is me. Me alone.'

For a few moments, the official was silent as he slowly formulated his next question in his mind. Suddenly, Mahesh decided to fill the empty air, helpfully volunteering a few facts. 'Shaving this morning was done by me. Me alone. Also combing my hair. All done by me.' He didn't get the job. After many more rejections, the small furniture factory hired him.

The girl on the train was quite mysterious. It was difficult to predict which train she would be on and when. Every day before getting on the train he made a resolution to speak to her and he committed to memory the first line he would speak to her. He never got the opportunity. One never knew when something totally unforeseen might happen and be life-changing. That was exactly what had happened at the railway station in Venice.

In Venice, when the Somali sat next to him on the bench and commiserated about the future, a person who looked like a messenger of god appeared before them. He wore expensive clothes and carried a briefcase like an important official. Almost as if he could read their thoughts, he asked, 'Would you like to work on a ship?'

Scarcely believing his good fortune, Mahesh replied, 'Sir, we have been wandering around ever since we left our country looking for this chance.'

The official opened his briefcase, pulled out some forms, and filled them out in his own language. He asked them to pay him 500 dollars each. Between them they had a total of 840 dollars which he begrudgingly accepted. They signed a promissory note stipulating that they would pay the rest of the money in a month. 'Stay here while I go to fetch the shipping agent,' the official said. He walked away and they never saw him again. That day Mahesh learned that even white people are capable of cheating.

'The biggest railway station in Italy is in Milan. Let's go there and something will turn up,' said the Somali. They got on to a train without a ticket and managed to reach Milan. Mahesh had never seen a station that vast. A sound akin to a tremendous downpour was always present. From this station, one could travel to any city in Europe. Trains travelling to

Barcelona, Zurich, Frankfurt and so forth kept coming and going in what looked like a huge carnival. Mahesh and the Somali sat on a bench and mapped out a plan for the future. They had no money and no knowledge of the local language. As Mahesh looked up, he noticed, exquisitely etched in the wall, figures of the twelve zodiac signs. He later learnt that those carvings had been done by an artist at the request of a benefactor a long time ago. The scales of Libra, his own sign, were in perfect balance. As he pondered what this might foretell about his future, the scraggy looking Somali pitifully wailed, 'I am going to die.'

The Somali spoke a tiny amount of English. Like the immigration officer in Greece, he had a stock of questions. For three days both of them starved. They had absolutely no money and they survived by drinking tap water. While talking, the Somali would suddenly grip his stomach and roll on to the floor. He would chase anyone he encountered and ply them with questions. One day he gathered a valuable piece of information. Six miles away there was a church and on certain days they provided food, specific food on specific days.

Each day they walked for two hours. The priest would dispense food through a hole in the wall. The first preference was for refugees who were white and then blacks. He realized that even when you begged for food, whites were superior. As they walked again for two hours and reached the station, the Somali would suddenly grab his stomach and wail, 'I am hungry' or 'I will be dead tomorrow.' He was always hungry and when he howled endlessly, it would make Mahesh go berserk. Sometimes the Somali jumped up suddenly, accosted a passenger and would demand information about where a train was going and how long it would take. His head was full of questions. If his house caught fire and someone dropped a rope from a helicopter, he probably wouldn't grab the rope without asking a hundred questions.

One day the Somali began to cry while eating the food given by the church. 'I didn't study. In our house the number of children was more than the number of books we had,' he said. His final words to Mahesh were: 'You should go back home. Otherwise you will die here.'

The next day, quite mysteriously, the Somali disappeared. It was not clear whether he took his own life or whether he jumped on a train and went to another country. The last image Mahesh had of the Somali was of him running after passengers, his frail shoulders shaking up and down. After six months of living in the station, Mahesh realized something. In this world no one could die of hunger. Somehow, at the last moment, help would come from somewhere. One day, looking up casually he was startled by a figure in the mirror. It was himself. His clothes hung loosely on a stick-like frame. At the Milan Station, where 500 trains per day carried 400,000 passengers from 24 platforms, he was almost asleep, when he heard a Tamil word spoken. He opened his eyes with a start and there stood in front of him a young girl, wearing a yellow scarf around her neck.

In Toronto, apart from the time he spent cutting timber,

Mahesh kept searching for the girl on the train. He thought about the last time he had seen her. On that day, the train was not crowded and when he had got on to the train, she was already seated. She was reading and had a gadget stuck inside her ear and was perhaps listening to some song. While her eyes and ears were occupied, her fingers kept turning the pages. Another four or five stations and she would get off. At any moment something unexpected could happen.

When the train stopped at the next station, a blind man with a dog got in. The dog pulled the man towards a vacant seat and the girl gave him her seat and moved to another one. At that moment, her cell phone fell to the floor and slid towards Mahesh. He jumped, picked it up and offered it to her. She moved her pouting lips ever so slightly and said 'thanks'. It was a soft voice, like the breath of a mouse, and her words seemed to disappear before reaching him. For a brief second her eyes looked directly at him and they appeared to be almost smiling. The memory of that moment kept him going for a whole week.

The girl who stood in front of him at the Milan station was a Tamil. 'Brother, take a look at this ticket. I have a visa and I need to go to Paris. My sister and her family are expecting me. Please put me on the right train.' Her passport, visa and ticket all seemed to be in good order. Her face had that healthy glow of someone who had grown up eating three meals a day. It was not like his starved face. 'Sister, buy a bun for me,' he said. She readily obliged. 'Who are you?' he asked. Her reply amazed him as he had never heard such a response before in his life. 'Our village has been taken over by the army,' she said. 'On the outside, I am a Tamil. Inside, there is a Sinhalese child growing.' After that neither one spoke. He made sure that she got on to the right train and wondered if she had reached her destination.

In Milan winter came very early that year. The birds that flew north had all returned to the south. It was a really harsh winter. The cold tormented both the exposed and covered parts of his body equally. The snow continued to fall from morning to evening. In the morning it was Wednesday, and in the evening it was still Wednesday. From above, Aries to Pisces watched him. One day, it seemed that Libra had some good news for him. He had not eaten lunch. An elderly woman strolled by, pushing a young girl on a wheelchair. The girl was very beautiful. She might even have been a film star. He looked at her feet and noticed the expensive-looking soft leather shoes. 'Such delicate footwear for someone who cannot walk,' he thought. As if reading his mind, the wheelchair swivelled around and came towards him. The young girl offered him a 1000 lira note. It was equal to about a dollar, adequate for two cups of tea. Without a moment's hesitation, he extended his hand and accepted it. After six months of stretching out his hands, he was getting quite used to it. The girl had thought he was a beggar. That whole night he cried, thinking about his plight, and finally decided that he would take his life the following day.

He thought about the Somali bent over with his head between his knees. The Somali often asked: 'Remember, the fierce hunger that came yesterday. Will it come again today?' If the Somali had been around, he would have given him some advice. Like a dog looking for a good place to die, Mahesh kept wandering around, searching for the right spot. When he went by a circus tent, someone came out and called, 'There is work here, are you willing?'

Without answering the question, he responded: 'Will you give me food?' He worked for the circus for two years, doing menial chores. With the money he had earned, he bought a forged passport and asked the person who had sold it to him where he could go. He said 'Canada' and that was how he came to Canada.

The teacher who taught him in his childhood used to say: 'You haven't lost. You have only postponed victory.' That day he had two victories. He waited with 200 others at the Scarborough Immigration Centre to become a Canadian citizen. He wore a pure white shirt, a custom-tailored jacket and polished shoes. The magistrate welcomed them. 'When you came here today, you did not have a country. When you leave you will have a country. Canada. Congratulations. Stand up, raise your right hand and take the following oath,' he said.

'I, Mahesh Kanagasabapathy, swear that I will be faithful and bear true allegiance to Her Majesty Queen Elizabeth the Second, Queen of Canada, Her Heirs and Successors, and that I will faithfully observe the laws of Canada and fulfil my duties as a Canadian citizen.'

When the 'O Canada' anthem was played, he noticed her. The same girl he had seen on the train was singing loudly. She was dressed in a very delicate and transparent sari, displaying the same pouting, inviting lips. Her parents were beside her. A small boy who might have been her brother held a Canadian flag. He looked at her, and she looked at him. His legs did not shake. A Canadian smile appeared on his lips. She too smiled. In all the countries, among all kinds of people, in all languages and in all bedrooms there is a phrase that is uttered at least once. He was ready with it on his lips.

He walked towards her.

seventeen

Pilgrimage

OUR SERVANT GIRL had run away. It happened during my childhood, but I remember it well. It was not the first time the girl had disappeared. It was something she did routinely. We were used to it.

She came to work for us after our father had gone to a village even poorer than ours, and struck a deal with her family for her services. They were in even more difficult circumstances than we were. He had shelled out sixty rupees in currency notes bearing the image of King George VI – quite an impressive sum of money in those days of the British regime – for her parents as an advance on her wages. The understanding was that two rupees would be deducted from her pay every month. By the third time she disappeared, not even half of the money had been recovered.

As usual Papa sent out his army in search of her. Uncle set out downtown on his motorcycle, which made majestic noises, as if dragging out pieces of thunder. He went out on this particular mission with an eagerness and haste far beyond what the situation warranted. It was almost as if he had been waiting for such an occasion to arise. The others too went in all the directions of the compass, each according to his ability and imagination. They looked a little like the legendary monkey army of the Ramayana that set off in search of the kidnapped Sita.

Mama had a three-month-old baby in arms, wriggling like a dark, giant worm. The baby had been named Thillainayaki, and there was a story behind her name. She was a gift from god granted to my parents, an answer to prayers offered at the Thillai temple. The contract with god was that if the baby was delivered safely, the temple would be rewarded with a silver cradle and a silver image of the baby. We were planning to visit the temple in the next couple of days to fulfil the vow.

But there was a hitch. Before we could go on our pilgrimage, we had to find the girl who had run away. Though she wasn't even thirteen years old yet, the day-to-day functioning of our entire household revolved around her. She ably handled a variety of tasks – chores set by my mother, my father, aunt and me. She had a phenomenal memory. She found whatever was lost and saw to it that it did not get lost again. She swept the house, drew water, cooked, washed the clothes and cleaned the pots and pans. And if she still had any spare time left, she lay down by the wooden stove whose embers had just died down.

I was very upset by her disappearance. If we did not find

the girl somehow, our temple trip would get postponed. Papa had said so. It would cause me great embarrassment at school, where my trip had already been announced. My little brother was beyond such worries. He spent his time playing with two marbles. One of them was unique, with white flowers on a sky blue background. He played a game of rolling them over, tossing them up and catching them in his palms. I had tried many times, in vain, to bag those marbles.

Being my younger brother, he always addressed me respectfully as 'Anna'. 'Please come, let's play a game of marbles, Anna,' he pleaded. He did not know how to play the game, but his desire to learn it was endless. 'You're little, what use do you have for marbles? Give them to me, good boy,' I cajoled. He put his hands to his ears and pleaded, 'Aiyo, Anna, please don't ask for them, not these marbles.' An ocean of kindness welled up in me, and I let him be.

Mama squatted with her legs folded and her hands on her head. By her side, on a small mat, was the black worm, the new baby. If you went anywhere near the baby, you caught the stench of neem oil. I thought it was not the proper time to approach Mama. My thoughts were centred on Ponni, the servant girl. I secretly pleaded with the Thillai god that the girl be caught soon.

Those were the days when my prayers were promptly answered. Ponni was found that very night. Uncle on the motorcycle was the one who found her. She had been seen roaming the downtown streets. The fact that she had walked the entire distance without a single cent on her would later be a topic of much debate among the people of the village. For the time being, Mama was really happy with the way things had turned out, but she didn't show it. She kept picking on Ponni, but the girl didn't say a word in reply. A scent of molten metal came from her body. She sat there shrivelled, arms folded, hair in disarray, and head buried in her knees. Her sobs, which came at twenty-second intervals, were the only discernible signs of life.

'How did you run away?' 'Who provoked you?' 'Did anyone lure you with other kinds of temptations?' All sorts of questions were thrown at her. She didn't say a word. Only to Mama's questions, 'Are you hungry? Do you want to eat?' did she nod her head. Mama served her food and she mixed portions of rice and curry and gobbled them up greedily. Mama said that she had never before seen anyone eat so much at one sitting.

After his meal, Papa smoked a cigar and had a discussion with Uncle. The trip to the Thillai temple was fixed for the following Monday. Papa reminded Uncle that Thambi's car should be rented for the trip. My joy was twofold because, in addition to the outing, I would have Monday off from school. I spent the intervening nights without sleep.

I did not expect all the others to wake up so early that Monday. When I opened my eyes, it seemed to be still midnight. But one look at my little brother and I could see that he had woken up much earlier, finished his bath and was all set for the journey.

Stealthily, I foraged in the pockets of the shirt he had just taken off, but he had remembered to remove the marbles from them. There they were, jingling in the pocket of his new shirt, the noise jarred in my ears. I lovingly called out to him, 'Little brother.' He quickly guessed my intentions and put his hands over his ears, saying, 'Aiyo, Anna.'

An appeal to Mama would not be of any use. She was feeding the black worm and, in the process, anointing the baby's entire body with milk. She saw me and said, 'You wicked boy, you aren't dressed and ready yet? Run, run and get ready, the car will be here soon.'

Ponni was surrounded by a variety of pots and other baggage. Like a miser counting her money, she was taking stock of the things again and again: 'Bronze cauldron, frying pan, new pot, rice, sugar, gram…' She was wearing a green half-sari and a blouse that had been stitched to the measurements of someone else. A stiff and starched cotton skirt was tied tightly with a tape at her waist. Her dark tanned face shone more than usual. When she saw me, she threw her arms out like a huge bird flapping its outspread wings and chased me away. I made a mental note of her act and decided to take up the issue with her at some future point.

Two cars were available for rent in our village. I was greatly pleased that Papa had ordered Thambi's car. It was a box-shaped Austin 7. Our village had been discussing the merits of this car for several months now, but today was the first day I was going to have the fortune of experiencing its wonders.

Hearing the sound of the car, I ran to the fence. A crowd had already gathered around the car. Thambi, the owner and driver, was wearing a very respectable hat with a brim. Though it looked ridiculous and did not really go well with my expectations of what a driver should wear, it did seem appropriate on the driver of the box-shaped Austin 7. It was said that Thambi had vowed not to remove it from his head as long as his head was on his neck. I wondered what feats he resorted to, to keep it on while he bathed or slept. There he was, smoking a beedi, leaning against the car. I decided right away that if ever I got to drive a car, I would wear such a hat and smoke a beedi as I leaned against my vehicle.

The car stood there like a lion, roaring impatiently. The two lights on its arched front mudguards were ready to beam light. On either side of the car were footboards to step on when getting into the car. It had rolling engine covers and a ball-shaped horn placed outside the driver's window that looked out of place. With its shiny black paint coated with white dust, it emitted a strange aroma, a mixture of dust and petrol. After a while, the engine died down; the car was silent.

I stood on my toes and peeped into the car. Its wide seats had the colour of dung. When a few others tried to peep in, I shooed them away. Some tiny finger had written Vathani in the dust of the glass at the back. Vathani was my classmate. I had closely guarded my love for her. But now it seemed to be out in the open. For the rest of the day, I pondered over the mystery of who had written her name, but the riddle remained unsolved.

In addition to the driver, nine of us were to travel in that car: three in front, five at the back and Uncle on the footboard; that was the proposed plan. By the time I tried to get in, the others had already grabbed their places – Mama, Aunt, Ponni and my little brother. The windows did not have glass panes. There were only canvas curtains that could be rolled up.

Ponni sat by the window and my little brother settled on her lap and looked at me guiltily. How could this fellow be allowed to usurp my window seat? I murmured, out of Papa's earshot, 'Get down, will you?' Ponni was holding on to him tightly. 'Anna,' my little brother started sobbing. 'Get down, you rogue!' After some prolonged haggling, a deal was struck. 'Anna, you sit by the window while we go to the temple; I'll sit there when we return,' he said. I agreed and grabbed the seat. Papa sat in front, unaware of our deal.

With a readiness that suggested that he was waiting for just this moment, Thambi, our driver, inserted an iron rod with handles the shape of an unfinished rectangle into a hole in the front of the vehicle and turned it with all his strength, using both his hands. The car shook and heaved. Ponni opened her mouth wide and my little brother giggled. On the third try, it let out a sound more appropriate to a car and the engine revved up. The driver put the rod away and climbed into his seat. Uncle hung on to the footboard outside and the car began its long journey.

I saw the whole world roll by. My little brother put his head between mine and Ponni's and peeped out too. That was against our deal and I rapped him hard on his head. That settled the matter.

167

I was in my own private world, enjoying the thrill of going so fast. Papa sat on the front seat and lit his cigar. Uncle hung on the footboard, holding on to the car with one hand, the other dangling, his hair askew, his upper cloth flapping in the wind, floating along very much like an angel. At that moment, my respect for Uncle increased tenfold.

On seeing our car approaching, carts pulled to the side, cyclists veered out of the way and made room for us. Load-bearers and pedestrians moved respectfully closer to the hedges on the side of the road. There were many others who just stood gaping in the direction of the car for minutes after we had passed by. The driver often blew on the ball-shaped horn to urge the pedestrians to keep out of our way.

The temple, however, was a big disappointment to me. It was a small one, inhabited apparently by a priest, a bull, a stray dog, and two beggars. We cheered up a little when we were told that more people would arrive at prayer time.

Mama spent all her time with the baby. It was left to Aunt and Ponni to take care of any preparations needed for the offering of milk rice to the god. It was quite late in the day by the time those items were ready for the offering. A few villagers joined us while the prayer was in progress. A little girl, dressed in a yellow silk skirt and red top, rather out of place with the shabbiness of the surroundings, came in. She ran about with her anklets tinkling. She had on her hair an enormous ball of stringed jasmine, almost as big as the one her mother wore. The girl attempted to play with the stray dog when her parents' attention was not on her. The dog

168

let out a growl in warning. Scared, she retreated, but then tried once again to get close to the dog. I eagerly awaited the moment when the dog's sharp teeth would meet her jewelled ankles. But I was deprived of this joy, because her father drove the dog away. It disappointed me to no end that a dog raised exclusively on temple food should get up and move away slowly, without even a growl of protest, or even the faintest effort to establish its loyalty to the temple.

Papa and Mama placed the custom-made silver cradle and baby-idol on a plate and gave it to the priest. My little brother and I took turns to ring the temple bell. After the prayer was said, banana leaves were spread on the floor and the milk rice was served. The hot rice darkened the banana leaves it was served on. We picked up morsels of it, from the edge of the leaves and had to blow on it to cool it down before we could eat it. Papa suggested that we rest until the heat of the day died down, and then make our way home.

I had not seen Mama this happy for quite a while. She sat in a cool sheltered spot inside the temple, her legs stretched out and she began to chew on betel leaves. Aunt sat by her side and Mama's mouth turned red from the betel leaf. She saw me and called out lovingly, 'You rogue, come here.' That day, her stretched-out neck swayed attractively and a languid smile appeared on her face. Before the smile could unfold completely and take on a definite shape, I slipped down and away from the platform.

Uncle was lying under the banyan tree with his legs folded and arms stretched out. He looked like a three-dimensional map. Papa sat near him, smoking a cigar. His eyes were closed as if he were in a trance. I could see the pores on his nose clearly. A slow, light blue smoke was coming out of his nose, dividing itself into two, like the slit tongue of a snake.

Assuming an innocent look, I went to where Ponni was squatting with her skirt pulled up to her thighs, gathered and tucked in. Her cheeks swelled and moved. From a distance, she looked like a frog resting with its legs stretched apart. As I neared her, I could see that she was muttering something. The sound was audible, but not the words. I listened a little more carefully and I recognized the popular Tamil song from the stage dramas that Ponni frequently sang. 'Steal I did the earring. Steal I did the earring. O, merciful god under the Maruda tree, steal I did a nose-ring too. But the nose was that of Muththambi's wife.'

She sang this over and over and never got tired of those lines.

She was washing the pots, one by one, with the kind of love and care one might display while bathing a baby. Her nails had cracked and looked like upturned half-moons. When she saw me she sulked as if she harboured a new-found anger. She tried hard to make sure that her back was turned towards me so that I could not look up her tucked-in skirt.

'Ponni, when are you going to run away to the town again?' I asked and moved away from her before she gave me a hateful look.

Like golden pollen, sand glistened on the ground. When

you placed your foot on the sand, your toes sank in. The grains shone in the sunlight. The stray dog chased a waterbird, its courage returned. The bird soared high, round and round, as if it were mopping up the sky. A beggar, whose skin appeared to hang loose over his skeletal frame, spread his left palm out like a lotus, plopped his lunch put on a banana leaf, and ate with his right hand.

I could not bear to watch that beautiful day go waste. My little brother was playing with his marbles. I went near him and, with my hands locked behind my back, said, 'Come.' He came to me instantly, collecting his marbles and thrusting them inside his pocket, as if I had invited him to come on a treasure hunt.

'Anna, my sweet brother, tell me, where are we going?'

'A very special place.'

'Aiyo, a special place!'

He hurried over, the marbles jingling in his pocket. His blue shirt ballooned in the wind like sails. He had chubby red cheeks and a large black dot on his forehead. He quickened his pace, as if he was about to set out on an important mission.

I stopped suddenly. In an overbearing voice, I asked, 'Will you tell on me?'

'No.'

'Sure you'll not speak?'

'Sure.'

I gave him a knock on his head to bring home the importance of the secret. He began to bawl, 'Ah, Ah!'

'Okay then, you devil, go back.'

He begged, 'Please, Anna, please.'

His pleading tone touched me. He walked on for some time, pondering something deeply, his head hanging low. Then he said, laughing, 'Look here.' Two marbles sat on his palm. He stretched his arm out and placed them in my hands.

'Are you serious?'

'Yes, yes. These are for you. You keep them.'

'You'll not want them back?'

'No, I'll not,' he promised.

Just as Karna in the great epic Mahabharata had given his armour to the enemy, my little brother gave away his marbles without a thought. I took the marbles from him and put them away safely in my pocket, unaware that he was to die in the next few minutes. When we came to the pond, I put my feet into the water. I said he could watch me from a distance. He did that.

'Don't come anywhere near.'

'No, I won't.'

Suddenly he asked, 'Anna, can you swim?'

It was as if he wanted me to be a master of all the arts of the world. I did not give a direct reply to his question. 'This pond is not very deep,' I said.

He moved a little closer.

'Don't come near me.'

'Let me just put my feet in, Anna.'

That was how he got his feet wet. There was a proud look in his eyes.

He shouted, 'Anna, look at me, look at me.'

I was wild. I did not want him to enjoy the water more than I thought he should. I had to be doing something more than he did, always.

'Look,' I said.

Then, right before my eyes, he began to slip down into the ankle-deep water. I stared at him, mesmerized, as if it were a dream. I could have easily just extended my hand to help him or raised a cry while he struggled in the water. I did not do either. I stood there completely stiff, for about a minute, watching the whirlpools that formed on the spot. I thought he would rise up as if by magic, clapping his hands and laughing. My memory is that I ran shouting loudly to Mama only after that.

Papa and Mama and Aunt lifted my little brother out and rushed him to the hospital in the car. Uncle gathered us together, packed our things and, carrying them on his head, brought us back home by bus. Soon after we had returned, the car also arrived. The people of the village had all somehow gathered at our house. Papa got down first. Like one carefully carrying a veena, the musical instrument made from seasoned jackwood, he carried my little brother in his arms, walked to the centre of the room and placed him on the cot there. All of a sudden, it felt as if all the air in the room had vanished. I left the room as I couldn't breathe any more.

My Papa and Mama were good people. Until the end, they never once interrogated me or asked me what had happened. I never told them how my little brother drowned or ever confessed my guilt. He had been playing happily by himself

173

with his marbles but I had enticed him to the pond and worse, I had not given him a hand when he was disappearing. I had stood there mesmerized, watching with curiosity the whirlpools of water forming above his head. All of this I never spoke about to anyone.

I also never disclosed to anyone that I was not able to live up to my promise of giving my little brother the window seat on the return journey in that Austin 7 box car, with its rolled-up canvas window.

eighteen

The Enemy

H E NEVER THOUGHT of himself as someone who could have enemies. But over a period of time, he came to have one; a real enemy, one worth the name. Strangely, it was not the kind of enemy one usually faces, such as a two-legged one; this enemy was a reptile: a snake.

The enemy had been at work for at least six months, trying to entice him into open war. But its activities had been so underhanded that he didn't even have an inkling of the first attack on his property. It was by sheer accident that one day, Mwange, while herding the chicks inside the coop for the night, saw two freshly laid eggs. Deciding to pick them up the next morning, he shut the coop door. But when he went for them the next day, the eggs had disappeared. He asked Emily if she knew anything about the eggs and she told him that she had not gone anywhere near the coop. He asked the neighbours in the adjoining huts, and they knew nothing

175

either. After four market-days, the pilfering happened again. The ground had become wet with a slight drizzle and there were marks on the ground, showing that a snake had crawled by. He decided to get rid of the snake somehow.

Killing snakes or even catching one was not an activity he particularly fancied. But then, he had not been fond of rearing hens either; he had been drawn into it by chance. He was a scholar with an education from a Christian school some 30 miles from Nairobi. He had successfully secured a senior certificate, second division, from that school, which was a matter of pride for him. He knew that his job was not commensurate with his education and intelligence. But he had walked in and out of companies, certificate in hand, and success had eluded him.

No one in the big companies had recognized his worth, so he had ended up at a milk depot, measuring and doling out milk. The work went smoothly for some time. He started quite early in the morning and went about it so vigorously he had no time to sit still. He received the milk, which began to arrive from six in the morning, measured it and poured it into huge tubs. There would be long queues of old people, young girls and boys waiting for the milk. Even as he attended to one line, another would form. He had to take care of both simultaneously. It was then that Mwange got the opportunity to use his senior-certificate, second-division brains. Emily Okinawa inspired him to do it. Tall, well built and with a child on her hip, she came to his booth to fetch milk every morning. Her swaying walk did something to his

176

heart. Whichever way she did her hair, she looked attractive: whether pushed to the back or front, tied up in a bun on top of the head, or made into umpteen braids, it looked beautiful. It was her beauty that had prompted him to steal.

Mwange was not specially known for his honesty. He had played football while at school and had maintained his physique. He was adept at scoring goals; his secret was that he had made a fair number of goals with his hands. He was a little liberal, too, with the milk he measured out to Emily, giving her two litres instead of one, not worried about the consequences. But one day he was caught in the act and fired.

His dismissal made him think about changing careers, and it occurred to him that he should start a chicken farm. He did not know the basics of running a chicken farm. What's more, chickens didn't seem too happy to be raised by him. He also knew this was not the work for a senior certificate, second division. Yet, he went into it thinking it would make him independent, not answerable to anyone, and he could keep the money he made for himself and perhaps move towards prosperity. There was a more immediate reason for his decision. Emily had told him that if he moved to the village and set up a farm, she would move in with him.

Indereko, who worked for him, knew the rudiments of chicken farming. Together, Mwange and Indereko worked hard, fed the birds, gave them water, spread sawdust inside the coops, swept and cleaned them, did all kinds of back-breaking work. As the old proverb goes, 'If you are having an affair with a woman on the other side of the river, you have to learn to swim.' The first six months went by without a hitch; that is, until the snake showed up. It seemed to be a clever one. However close Mwange pulled the wire mesh together, the snake successfully gained entry into the coop. Its ways were, indeed, mysterious. Mwange and Indereko toiled endlessly, but all their hard work with the chickens was in vain. The snake grew fat and acquired an enviably shiny skin. It nourished itself with frequent meals of eggs and with the occasional chicken, perhaps whenever it felt it needed protein supplements.

The fever tree, with its yellow, shiny bark, grew in marshy places near the farm. Mwange broke one branch from the tree to use in a face-off against the enemy. The branch was sturdy, easy to handle and pliable, and he knew he would not find a better weapon to combat the snake. He kept it by his bedside. He practised different fencing attacks, waving it vigorously in the air. He stroked it, comforted it and kept it with such good care that the stick was always ready for a fight.

Emily did not share the devotion Mwange had for his stick. Her two-year-old had taken to running outside the house to play and she was forever scared that the snake might harm her baby. Yet, she did not like Mwange venturing out stealthily, at night, torch in one hand and fever-tree stick in the other, as if challenging the snake to a face-to-face duel. The thought that some harm might come to him if he accidentally stepped on the snake made her cringe in fear. Mwange was not one to listen to her words. Saving his birds was no longer the issue. He had to take revenge on his enemy; he had to slay the snake. That had become the sole preoccupation and purpose of his life. But he had yet to set eyes on the snake – his declared arch-enemy! Nor did the snake seem to be very keen on meeting him. Mwange only saw the trail of the snake and empty chicken coops.

The two enemies, however, came face to face one day. It was Joseph, his neighbour, who first sighted the reptile. He shouted to Mwange. Perhaps the snake had got tired of idling away its time and lazily feeding on eggs. It had come slowly out to bask in the warmth of the morning sun. Mwange, for a minute, stood admiring the crawler. How indolent it was, how nonchalant and unhurried, as if saying, 'Why not wait until tomorrow to settle our differences?'…Mwange rushed into his house and came out with the fever-tree stick held high above his head, and like a Maasai warrior waved it in all directions. The snake understood that Mwange's intentions were anything but honourable. It lifted up its hood and hissed. Its beady eyes shone. They looked rather big for its small head. It put out its red, forked tongue as if testing the air. It spread its hood and put on a regal appearance. Suddenly, prompted by unknown considerations, it shrank its body and crept into a pile of bricks. It failed to give the respect due to an enemy, who was its equal and ignored him.

Mwange thought perhaps he had made a grievous mistake. His behaviour towards the snake was rather uncivilized. It was unarmed and here he was, swinging his stick and madly running around the brick-pile. The snake slowly crawled through to the other side of the pile and slithered away among the cactus bushes. The reason for Mwange's frenzied running was because he thought the snake might be a spitting cobra. One needed special skills to beat a spitting cobra. It targeted the victim's eyes and from a distance spat venom that could make one blind. So he was hoping to attack its tail. Later he realized that the snake was not a spitting cobra. The first day of the battle ended disastrously for Mwange.

The next day Mwange found that the snake had eaten an egg and spat out the shell. He did not have to tear his curly hair wondering how many eggs had been stolen. From then on, the snake, as if marking its attendance, left a clear count of the eggs it had pilfered by spitting out the shells. Mwange was ashamed and doubled his efforts to nab the snake.

He could not sleep until very late that night. His thoughts were on the reptile. In that stifling small room, he lay on the cot covered with a cowhide blanket. By his side was Emily. Even in the darkness he could see the even rise and fall of her breasts. The scent of her warm body heat wafted from her side. Her breath smelt of the porridge she had eaten and was a little stronger than normal. It took him some time to find the knot of her *lasa* and tug at it. She groaned, 'Vacha, vacha,' and turned over to accommodate him. Her hand fell by chance on his thigh. That was what he liked in her. She never refused and would lovingly scold him, saying, 'The generous woman is always pregnant.'

Emily's son was now two years old, and they had planned to get married when he became four and they had saved up enough money. Emily wanted a grand wedding. She wanted

180

to wear a white dress, veil, long silk gloves and walk like an angel down the aisle to bridal music. She delighted in imagining their son leading the procession with a bouquet in his hand. She had saved a respectable amount of money. If Mwange could also save a little, they could have a grand wedding the way she wanted. It seemed the snake was determined not to let that happen.

An idea came to Mwange. The snake was fourteen feet long. How swift it was, and with such sharp green eyes! Was it not the satiny-smooth black mamba of Africa? That snake could climb trees. It climbed trees and entered houses through the roofs. What was the use in sealing the holes in the doors and the mesh? Once again he went out with his torch, fully armed. That snake was definitely the biggest challenge of his life and he had tried nearly all the tricks he knew. He had cut down all the low-hanging branches; he had poured kerosene oil all around the trees. He had tarred the trees, nailed sharp tins on them and left the lights burning right through the night. Still the snake eluded him. It seemed to know all the tricks that men played. Mwange was now tired and at the end of his tether. It was then that it struck him that his neighbour, Joseph, might be able to help. He knew all about snakes and was sure to have a solution.

These days Emily was afraid to stay alone in the house. She was afraid for her son. A black mamba was very poisonous. When bitten by it, death occurred within minutes. She thought Mwange was not really serious about killing the snake and had not acted as quickly as he should have. That made her angry, and she threw a tantrum. The kitchen floor shook. Her lips quivered. She had spread out her legs like a pair of scissors. Her hands were busy cutting the marinda spinach. Mwange tiptoed to her and sat by her side. He caught her hand and she resisted him.

'My priceless woman, my sweet fragrance, please look at me. The water that is hot will cool in time. I shall certainly kill the snake one of these days. Just be a little patient,' he pleaded. But she was adamant. 'I want my son to live. I see him go to bed at night. My mind trembles when I think of whether I will see him alive in the morning. Is such drama necessary? I have entrusted my son to the Almighty. I have spoken enough, I have no more words. My salutations to you, Kabisa.' The words fell from her mouth strong and sure as the judge's hammer. Mwange stroked her ears. Just when she began to groan he embraced her. Her shoulders were stiff and unyielding. Her upper lip was thick and tasty, but she wrinkled her nose and pretended to resist him.

Finally Joseph came up with a plan. It was simple and economical. He suggested that Mwange buy four ping-pong balls and mix them up with the eggs. The plastic balls would look exactly like eggs and not knowing the difference the snake would swallow the balls. It was a foolproof method that the villagers always used. Joseph was confident that the snake would be duped and stopped. And so that is what they did. That night Mwange made a few forays outside to see if he could find the snake. But he saw nothing and slept late and woke up only after the sun had fully risen. Emily had already gone to work with her son. A chilly wind blew. The jacaranda tree had covered the ground with its flowers, colouring the yard violet. He went around his chicken coop and thought he saw something different. Two balls had gone and his heart began to beat faster. He was excited and searched all over the place. He looked in all the probable places the snake might have gone. He was not sure that the snake would be so easily deceived. He went past the fever tree to the place where the elephant grass began, and then he saw it – the dead snake. It was completely and thoroughly dead and lay there long, black and shining. Its small mouth was torn open and blood oozed out of it possibly from banging its head on the ground. Ants were all over the reptile. Two bulges could be seen in the neck. How long it looked! Its head was also smashed and the tail was still moving slightly.

People from the neighbouring huts came to look at the snake. Seeing the tail move, each one of them took a hit at it. The children had a field day. They looked wide-eyed at Mwange and then began to sing: 'Mwange is a great hero. The brave one who killed the snake.'

Okilo, the village messenger, came running from some-where. No funeral procession was complete without him. He picked up the snake and wore it around his neck as a garland. Its head and tail trailed on the ground. Okilo did a death dance, his arms spread out and knees half bent. The children followed him beating on boxes, tin cans and the procession went around the huts several times.

The elders praised Mwange; some spoke expansively of

his cleverness. It was natural for a snake to feed on eggs. Now it dangled unceremoniously around Okilo's neck and was dragged in a most undignified manner over the dusty ground.

Later, the long shining body of the snake kept coming up in Mwange's mind. In a just war that was fought between two equals, somehow wile and deceit had entered the machinations. What was so great about this victory? he wondered. Mwange sat on his haunches outside his hut for a long time. He was there even after Emily and her son came back. Sensing something was wrong, she quickly put her son down on the ground and hurried to him. He could not look her straight in the face. He stood up and threw away the strong, pliable fever-tree stick. Mwange, senior certificate, second class, then entered the house, his head bowed.

nineteen

The American Girl

ONE DAY SHE had a boyfriend, the next day she did not. He had gone his way, looking for another girl. To date, this was her third boyfriend. She didn't seem to understand how to attract these boyfriends, let alone how to hold on to them. Maybe she didn't possess that certain charm they were looking for. Or even if she possessed it, she failed to give it away; that much was clear.

She was indeed a beautiful girl, although she neither wore make-up, nor adorned herself particularly. She didn't have time for such things. She dressed just like other students, but you couldn't say she sounded like them. She had come to an American university on a scholarship, directly from Jaffna, Sri Lanka, and so her pronunciation was off. In addition, she used several words which other American students could not understand. She said 'sweet' while they said 'candy'; she said 'lift' while they said 'elevator'; she said 'torch' while they said 'flashlight'. All this, though, was only when she first arrived; she corrected herself very quickly. She didn't use her intelligence in just pursuing subjects like chemistry, physics and mathematics.

Men were drawn to her, anyway, like swarms of ants, attracted by her long dark hair and her darting black eyes. But then they turned away with the same haste. Or else they abandoned her and fled to other girls. To this day, she remembered with shock the very first question put to her by the very first young man who approached her. 'Why do you always stand with your head bent, as if someone were playing the national anthem?' he asked. How was she to answer this? For seventeen years she had walked to school and back in that stance, looking down at her feet. She couldn't change that, all of a sudden. But she liked the boy who posed the question. They were taking some of the same courses, and he would join her as she walked to her class.

He invited her to attend a basketball game one day. She had no idea about the rules; she only knew that the ball had to land inside the basket. There were many girls wearing short skirts which showed their thighs, and long red socks, who jumped up and down enthusiastically, cheering. Sometimes they clapped their hands even when the ball did not fall in the basket. So she, too, clapped her hands. On their way back, he bought her an ice cream. When a tiny bit dripped on to her lower lip, he wiped it away with a finger. On the third day, he invited her to study together with him. She was stunned by the sharpness of his mind. Unlike her, he never learnt

186

anything by rote. He thought things through logically, and could work out the most complicated chemical equations in no time. Three days later, he told her his roommate was away and invited her to stay the night in his room. When she refused, he vanished and was not seen again.

The second guy to come after her was daring, a bit of a prankster. She knew the atomic structure of benzene; he did not. That was how their friendship began. One day he appeared suddenly and stood in front of her as she was studying. When his shadow fell on her and she looked up, he gave her swivel chair a spin. It whirled round three times and came to a stop directly in front of him. He said, 'Look, I've drawn the prize! Now you have to come and have coffee with me.' She wanted to laugh; she agreed. As they were drinking their coffee, he asked her, 'Are you a princess in your country?'

'No,' she told him, 'I was actually driven away from there. I have to find a country for myself after my studies.'

'You are as beautiful as a princess,' he assured her and asked whether he could stay in her room that night. Before she could say anything, he too disappeared.

All these people wanted something from her. But although she lived in America, she remained a Sri Lankan. No one here knew that even before she left for America, the people of her village used to call her the 'American Girl'. She had even forgotten her own name. Both at home and at school, everyone called her the 'American Girl'. Her mother used to say she was smarter than her two elder brothers. She had learnt to speak English at the early age of four. She would read all the American comic books that her brothers brought home, and relate the stories to her classmates at school. She'd dream that she had turned into Superman or Archie, and lived in America.

Even as a young child, she'd ask her mother, 'Am I an American Girl, really?'

'No,' her mother would reply, 'You are Sri Lankan.'

'Then when can I become an American?'

'You can't.'

'If I go to America will I become an American?'

'No, you'll still remain Sri Lankan.'

'What would happen if I married an American?'

'Then you'd be a Sri Lankan girl married to an American. Whatever you do, you can never turn yourself into an American.'

She was deeply disappointed on hearing this. She was ten years old at that time.

The third person to fall in love with her was a boy who was wealthy. She was, by then, a second year student. He approached her directly as she was coming out of a class and introduced himself. At once, several girls turned to look at her with jealous eyes. He told her he lived in a student hostel and visited his parents in Portland every weekend.

He had a novel way of getting out of his car. Having stopped the car, he'd thrust both legs out at the same time, stand up and then step forward. He never seemed to concern himself with the lessons that had gone yesterday or were on today, nor the lessons that were to come tomorrow. He seemed to think that the entire university was a playing field. He followed her everywhere. One day he asked her to close her eyes. He usually did this whenever he brought her a present, so she did as she was told. 'Open your mouth,' he said. She opened her mouth, thinking he was going to give her a piece of chocolate, or some kind of candy. She used to open her mouth in exactly the same way when her mother gave her medicine. Instead, he bent down and kissed her open mouth. She didn't like this one bit.

'It's no big deal,' he said. 'I've kissed your hand. I've kissed your forehead. Your mouth is just two inches lower than your forehead. So let's say this was an error of two inches.' He invited her to his home for Thanksgiving dinner. The previous year, she had gone to her friend's home. She accepted his invitation, since there would be no one at all in her hostel on Thanksgiving Day, and travelled for two hours with him, in his car. This was her longest car journey in America so far.

His parents were very respectable. Although his father looked middle-aged, his mother appeared much older. Her face was criss-crossed with lines, like a wooden block at the fishmonger's. Having found out somehow that her son's girlfriend was a Sri Lankan, the old lady had collected a number of newspaper clippings, all to do with recent events in Sri Lanka, which she now handed to her. Her heart was touched by this. At the dinner table, the conversation was all about the war in Sri Lanka. It was two years since the Indian Army had arrived in her country. She told her hosts how her mother had moved to three different locations during this time, and how she had to keep changing the addresses when she wrote to her Mom. She did not mention that her two brothers had died during the conflict.

That evening, before he went upstairs, the boy pulled out the sofa-bed and told her she was to sleep there. She fell into a deep sleep. At around midnight, a soft hand closed her mouth gently. She opened her eyes to see him standing there. She was terrified. She began to shake all over, and her nightdress was soaked through with sweat. Although she managed to drive him away, she did not sleep a wink for the rest of the night. The next day, she spoke no more than two sentences during the entire two hours they travelled together in the car.

It was at the end of her third year that her university life saw a great change. She had allowed two years to pass by without participating in the annual multicultural event. That year, though, she could not avoid it. She was the only student from Sri Lanka. She named her contribution, 'A Traditional Dance'. She didn't have a single sari with her, nor any other appropriate dance costume. She borrowed some clothes from a Punjabi friend and got ready, making herself up as best as she could.

She had decided to dance to a song she had once performed at school, 'Enna thavam seidanai?' ('What penances did you do?'). She had already recorded the song on to a tape. The curtains slid away as she stood on stage. Although she was trembling slightly, she explained the song in a couple of lines and proceeded to dance. She didn't expect the enthusiastic applause that followed, the students cheering and clapping.

Just before her performance, a Vietnamese student had sung, accompanying himself on a stringed instrument. When she came out, having washed off her make-up, he praised her dancing extravagantly. For the sake of conversation, she, in her turn, said his music had been wonderful. He told her that he had learnt to play the sixteen-stringed instrument, usually reserved for women, from his Vietnamese mother. He said he played it occasionally, and in memory of her. She was amused by what he was wearing: a long robe covered in a thousand mirrors, and a round cap on his head. His clothes reflected a thousand tiny images of her. He was a third year student of English Literature, and said his name was Lan Hing.

The next morning, Lan Hing somehow managed to seek her out in that university of 27,000 students. 'You never told me your name yesterday,' he said.

'Mathi,' she replied.

He asked her surname.

In three years, no one had asked what her surname was. She wanted to laugh. She said, 'I have a very long surname. It will take you half a day to learn it by heart.'

'Really? What does "Mathi" mean in your language?'

She told him it had two meanings: 'intellect' and 'moon'.

'The moon is very sacred to the Vietnamese, it has a special place in all our festivals,' he said. He went on, 'Your dance yesterday was very beautiful. The movements were very similar to the Vietnamese style of dancing.'

'Is that so? Thanks,' she said.

191

'You included some movements like a baby crawling. Why was that?'

She wasn't sure whether he really wanted to know, or whether he asked it merely to keep the conversation going. All the same, she explained, 'It was a story of a mother and child. Unable to bear the pranks of her crawling child, the mother tied him momentarily to a stone mortar.'

He, unlike her, had grown up in America. When she narrated the story, he said, 'Really? That mother was fortunate she wasn't born in America.' Laughing and displaying his large teeth, he added, 'If any mother here were to tie up a child to a stone mortar, she would be arrested and put in prison.' She couldn't stop laughing at that. He looked at her eyes in surprise, as if seeing them for the first time. Her eyes seemed to laugh even before her mouth began to smile.

It was a matter of surprise to her that even after their third or fourth meeting, he didn't ask to stay the night in her room. This really pleased her. She didn't know why, but it felt very natural to be with him. She didn't have to make any sort of effort when she sat with him, or walked about with him, or talked to him. She didn't have to try in any way to please him. In his presence, somehow, her heart beat differently.

She used to write to her mother every month. Her mother didn't have access to a telephone in the village where she now lived. So every two or three months she would go to a nearby town, telephone her daughter and speak to her for three minutes. Her call would come precisely at 6 o'clock. The blue aerogramme that her mother wrote arrived regularly as well.

That month the army had slaughtered many people in their home village of Kokkattisolai. The mother didn't say a word about it. When Mathi wrote at the end of that month, she finished with these lines, 'Amma, I was born your daughter, but I've done nothing at all for you. I haven't even bought you a single thing that you wanted. Yesterday I bought myself some shoes for the winter. They cost me forty dollars. Had I sent you the money, it would have seen you through your household expenses for three months. I was the "American Girl" only while I was there. Here I am a Sri Lankan. I have made friends with a man who has a strange name. Lan Hing. There is only one such name in the entire telephone directory. He is a good man. I must see you again. Don't die before I do that.'

A phrase that Lan Hing often used was, 'Surprise me!' They would go out to dinner in the evenings. She'd ask him what they should order. 'Surprise me,' he'd say. They'd decide to go to the cinema. 'What movie shall we watch?' she'd ask. 'Surprise me,' he'd say. One day when Lan Hing came looking for her, she was doing some work on her computer and took no notice of him. He watched her for a long time. Her fingers were very narrow and slender. He gazed at them as they played swiftly upon the keyboard. He told her that when her fingers touched the keys, there was still so much space left on the keys. As he said this, he took one of her fingers in his hand and stroked it. Who knows what struck her but she stood up suddenly and kissed his large toothed mouth.

Another evening after it had rained, she sat in the shade

of a birch tree, thinking of her mother. A picture came to her mind of her mother getting ready to teach at her school, shaking out her sari and putting it on, tying up her hair in a knot with a hair-net around it, setting off finally with her umbrella. As she wondered whether it was raining at home, too, Lan Hing appeared, his shoes squelching through the wet earth. When he saw a puddle of water, he leapt across it like an ancient warrior and landed in front of her.

'Such a big leap to cross such a small puddle,' said Mathi. She looked very lovely in a clinging, transparent dress. He bent down to touch her and remarked, 'Today your skin is even softer than your feather-like dress.'

'Is it? Today I'm not going to surprise you. Why don't you surprise me for a change?' she said.

'Do you know what I learnt in English Literature today?'

'I will know if you tell me.'

'The Russian novelist Tolstoy had thirteen children. Did you know that?'

'No, I didn't. Tell me more.'

'The thirteenth child was a boy. Do you know what Tolstoy did when the child was dying? He was learning to ride a bicycle. He was sixty years old at the time.'

'Why are you telling me this?'

'You told me to surprise you, that's why.'

Slowly she began to smile.

'Look, look, your eyes have started to laugh.'

She began to study for a doctorate, while he finished his graduate degree and accepted a teaching post. When he rented a small one-room apartment, they decided to live together. She moved in with him, bringing her bed and her desk, and all her other belongings. They had a civil wedding first, after which he put around her neck the thaali her mother had sent, strung on a chain. 'Aren't there any appropriate Vietnamese rituals?' she asked. So on a full moon night, with the old man in the moon as witness, he bit into a piece of ginger dipped in salt, ate part of it, and she ate the rest. With this, their married life began grandly, blessed by the man in the moon.

From the day they were married, she abandoned the use of a pillow. She became accustomed to sleeping with her head against his upper arm as he lay on his slightly higher bed. Lan Hing looked after all the household jobs as well as holding down a teaching position. He was a splendid husband. But there was no way he could keep the house tidy, however hard he tried. Her reference books, notebooks and scraps of paper on which she had scribbled notes lay scattered everywhere, on the bed, in the kitchen, in the bathroom, on her desk. He never ceased to wonder how on earth she managed to study. He would spend a couple of hours cleaning the house and putting everything away tidily, but within minutes she would scatter her things again.

For her PhD, she had to spend a long time in the laboratory. Sometimes she worked for twenty hours at a stretch. All the same, she wrote to her mother every month without fail. 'Amma, do you know something? Even when I was an embryo in your womb, I already had embryos in mine. So any baby that is born to me will actually have come directly from you.'

One Saturday afternoon, she didn't go to the laboratory. She had finished her research and was at the point of finishing her thesis. Lan Hing came into the bedroom and stood still. The dirty plates from breakfast had not been removed. She was bent over her notebook and writing something in it. A half-drunk mug of coffee was in her lap. Lan Hing pushed away some books from the bed to make space, sat down, removed the mug of coffee and took her hands. 'You are the finest student in the entire world, there is no doubt about it. But although we have been married for four years, we still don't have a child. You should think about that, too. Let us consult a doctor.' Silently she gazed up at him. His cheekbones were sticking out distinctly; she had not noticed that before.

The doctor subjected both of them to extensive tests, and came to a conclusion which they had not expected at all. Her husband, who had always said, 'Surprise me, surprise me', got the biggest surprise of his life on the day they learnt the results of the medical examination. The doctor went inside to fetch the results. As the sound of his shoes retreated, their heartbeats grew louder and louder. 'In order to conceive a baby, a man should have a sperm count of at least twenty million per millilitre. Yours wasn't even half that,' the doctor said. There was no possibility of her becoming pregnant by him.

The two of them, who had thought all these days that it

would be pleasant to have a child, were now in frenzy to have a baby, somehow or the other. Mathi's mother's letters began to ask, 'Are you pregnant yet?'

He asked her one morning as she was lying in bed at his right side as usual, 'Hey, Sri Lankan girl, why did you marry me?'

She responded, 'A rich girl will marry a rich man, a poor girl seeks a poor man. An educated girl goes for an educated man; those who have nothing marry each other.' Her mouth smiled, but her expression revealed an unbearable grief.

'Look here, I didn't tie you with the thaali so you could be chained to me like a pen at a post office. If you like, I will leave you. Please marry someone else and have a baby.'

She said nothing, but moved swiftly up to his bed, pulled his arm towards her and lay down, pressing her head against it even harder than usual.

Throughout those weeks, on every channel on the television, the Clinton–Lewinsky affair was being discussed. The same thing was transmitted on radio. The newspapers covered it endlessly. Nothing caught her attention. In the evening she sat in her room, gazing out of the window at the street outside. She had submitted her thesis three days earlier, so her mind wandered. A police van raced past, its siren sounding. She didn't know how she would spend all the hours of the day hereafter. Footsteps sounded suddenly, along the street. Students, boys and girls, were coming from a basketball match. One young man walked, carrying a girl on his shoulders. Everyone looked so joyful. She couldn't make out who had lost and who had won. In the kitchen, Lan Hing was clattering the dishes as he made her a Vietnamese soup. Its aroma wafted towards her. When he came out, bringing a bowl of soup, wrapped in his robe, he found her asleep in the chair.

The next day the two of them discussed the situation and came to a decision. They would use their entire savings to investigate the chances of conceiving a baby through IVF. An African colleague from his school offered to be their sperm donor. The doctor had to do many tests and it took six months to prepare her. She had to have twenty-eight injections of hormones and three days after her period ended, the embryo created in a laboratory was inserted into her. As soon as her pregnancy was confirmed, she wrote a letter to her mother. 'I am pregnant. Soon you will have news of the birth of a grandson or granddaughter. Wait.'

She was beset by many doubts. One day she asked her doctor, 'What exactly will the baby be, if it is born to a Sri Lankan and Vietnamese couple using the sperm donated by an African?' The doctor answered without any hesitation, 'It will be an American.'

In exactly two hundred and eighty days, a beautiful baby was born to her. It was an easy childbirth. She took out the paper and pen she had brought in her handbag, all ready, and wrote just one line to her mother. 'I have given birth to an American baby.' She gave it to her husband and asked him to mail it immediately.

That letter, with its stamp on the right hand corner of the

envelope, would somehow miraculously reach her mother whose address had neither a house number nor a street name. That whole day her mother would walk up and down the entire village, holding up the letter so that its American stamp was clearly visible to everyone.

Twenty days later, exactly at 6 o'clock, her mother telephoned. It was just as she expected. Her mother would have woken up at five in the morning to make that call. She would have caught the first bus to town, waited outside the telephone office, entered before anyone else, as soon as the doors opened.

The twenty-day-old baby lay on her lap. She heard her mother's voice, 'Daughter, what sex is the baby, you didn't say.'

'It's a girl, Amma, a baby girl. Amma, can you hear her crying?' She lifted up the baby and held her to the phone.

'Daughter, what have you named her?' She didn't hear her mother's voice, only the sound of her breathing.

'Amma, she's an American girl, through and through. You must see her. Don't die before you do that.'

They both spoke at the same time, their voices crashing somewhere above the Atlantic Ocean.

It seemed to her that the baby lying on her lap had exactly the same features as her mother. Her hair grew in tight curls all over her small head. When she grew older, she too would tie her hair in a knot like her mother and cover it with a hairnet. She'd go to a basketball match with her friends, wearing a short skirt and clap her hands at the right moments. She would not run away if her boyfriend invited her to stay the night in his room. At a multicultural event, she might dance to the song, 'What penances did you do?' Or she might play a sixteen-stringed instrument. Or she might do something American, like sing in a rock band. On Thanksgiving Day she would bring home a new boyfriend and introduce him to her parents. She would make sure, well ahead, that his sperm count was not lower than twenty million per millilitre.

Some other titles from the
RATNA TRANSLATION SERIES

The Sixth Finger
by MALAYATOOR RAMAKRISHNAN
Translated from Malayalam by Prema Jayakumar

A Faceless Evening and other stories
by GANGADHAR GADGIL
Translated from Marathi by Keerti Ramachandra

If A River and other stories by KULA SAIKIA
Translated from Asamiya

On A River's Bank by A. MADHAVAN
Translated from Tamil by M. Vijayalakshmi

Havan by MALLIKARJUN HIREMATH
Translated from Kannada by S. Mohanraj

Echoes of the Veena by R. CHUDAMANI
Translated from Tamil by Prabha Sridevan

Here am I and other stories by P. SATHYAVATHI
Translated from Telugu

Sripantha's Kolkata
Translated from Bangla by Anita Kar

www.ratnabooks.in